The Whole Animal

CORINNA
CHONG

THE WHOLE
ANIMAL

stories

ARSENAL PULP PRESS
VANCOUVER

THE WHOLE ANIMAL
Copyright © 2023 by Corinna Chong

ARSENAL PULP PRESS
Suite 202 – 211 East Georgia St.
Vancouver, BC V6A 1Z6
Canada
arsenalpulp.com

The publisher gratefully acknowledges the support of the Canada Council for the Arts and the British Columbia Arts Council for its publishing program, and the Government of Canada and the Government of British Columbia (through the Book Publishing Tax Credit Program) for its publishing activities.

Arsenal Pulp Press acknowledges the xʷməθkʷəy̓əm (Musqueam), Sḵwx̱wú7mesh (Squamish), and səl̓ilwətaʔɬ (Tsleil-Waututh) Nations, custodians of the traditional, ancestral, and unceded territories where our office is located. We pay respect to their histories, traditions, and continuous living cultures and commit to accountability, respectful relations, and friendship.

This is a work of fiction. Any resemblance of characters to persons either living or deceased is purely coincidental.

The following stories were previously published in different form: "The Whole Animal" in *Room* 38.3; "Zora, in the Whirl" in *Grain* 48.3; "Kids in Kindergarten" on CBC Books; "Fixer" in *Riddle Fence* #40; "Wolf-Boy Saturday" in *The Humber Literary Review* 4.1; "Old Wives" in *Grain* 38.3; "Porcelain Legs" in *Ricepaper* 18.4 and in *AlliterAsian: Twenty Years of Ricepaper Magazine* (Arsenal Pulp); "Thieves" in *Cosmonauts Avenue* June/July 2017; "Love/Cream/Heat" as "Love Cream Heat" in *The Fiddlehead* #293; "the snare. the arm. the guinea pig. the bottle. the bus. the night." in *PRISM international* 59.3.

The story of blue tits recounted in "Thieves" was drawn from an interview with Rupert Sheldrake, broadcast on CBC Radio's *Ideas* on January 24, 2008.

Cover and text design by Jazmin Welch
Cover art by Christina Mrozik, *Cebu Flowerpecker*, 2018, 13.5″ × 10.5″, watercolour and graphite on paper
Edited by Catharine Chen
Proofread by Alison Strobel

Printed and bound in Canada

Library and Archives Canada Cataloguing in Publication:
Title: The whole animal : stories / Corinna Chong.
Names: Chong, Corinna, author.
Identifiers: Canadiana (print) 2022041260X | Canadiana (ebook) 20220412642 |
   ISBN 9781551529158 (softcover) | ISBN 9781551529165 (EPUB)
Classification: LCC PS8605.H654 W56 2023 | DDC C813/.6—dc23

For Andrew

What I like about these dog bones is their ambiguity. It takes you a while to figure out what they are—maybe you don't figure it out. If it doesn't have ambiguity, don't bother to take it.

—SALLY MANN, PHOTOGRAPHER

CONTENTS

The Whole Animal

IT OPENED WITH A CLOSE-UP ON A SLAB OF BEEF. A vast red landscape, leaking blood from every fissure. As the camera slowly zoomed out, the red pool spilling over the edge of the plate came into view. The bleat of a calf cut through the thrum of timpani. Then, the meat began to take shape, its outlines edging into the frame, until it became clear that it was not just a T-bone steak, but also a map—the familiar silhouette of the United States of America. The title pounded across the screen, letter by letter: CARNIVORE NATION.

Ward snuggled into Ruby's chest, and she held his head as she would a frightened child's.

◆

Ward had been a vegetarian briefly, before he even knew Ruby. Ever since they met he'd been saying that he wanted to go back to it eventually, do it more responsibly this time. And yet, at least once a week, he'd been proclaiming his hankering for a big juicy burger, once even going to the grocery store at 10 p.m. to buy hamburger meat, no bun necessary. Upon discovering that all the ground beef was sold out, he'd instead purchased a chipotle-marinated beef tenderloin, then cooked and eaten the whole thing for a midnight snack. But that evening, as the credits rolled across the screen, his eyes shone like Christmas baubles at the prospect of cutting out meat—zero meat, presumably in perpetuity. Ward, like a puppy chasing his own tail.

The documentary had armed them with pocketfuls of facts on the dangers of eating meat, the cruel and unsustainable practices of animal farming, the ill effects of dairy. A whole-food vegan diet worked miracles, according to the film's guinea pig participants, who were suffering diabetes, high cholesterol, and the gamut of other twenty-first-century afflictions until they stopped eating meat. At one point during the film, Ruby had said, "I don't think I can ever eat a chicken breast again," and really believed herself. By the time they got to the denouement, she had been caught up in the film's shiny promise of renewal. She even found herself tearing up as she watched a formerly bedridden middle-aged woman chase and play Frisbee with her grandkids.

"Let's do it," she'd said to Ward.

She regretted her suggestion as soon as she'd uttered it. The next day, she insisted they buy a full bird and make her mother's famous roasted chicken for one last hurrah before jumping into veganism head-on. The chicken flesh turned out juicy, the skin crispy. Ruby shucked out the tenderest chunks of meat on the underside of the body—the oysters, her mother called them—and gave them one each, to be saved for the very last bite. She almost cried as it slid down her throat like butter.

"Where does the word *vegan* come from?" she asked, scraping at the grease on her plate. "What does it mean? Was it just that *vegetarian* was taken?"

"I guess." Ward shrugged. He'd left his skin on the edge of his plate like a pile of dead leaves. "*Vegan* is kind of minimized."

What it meant was food at its very barest. Food stripped down. They would become foragers, like ancient cave people.

"What about goat's milk?" said Ruby.

"Nothing from animals." Ward made a round shape with his hands, as though this were the universal symbol for animal. Whole.

"I read that goat's milk is more digestible than cow's milk," Ruby continued.

Ward just looked at her. Then, after enough silence had passed, he said, "Are we going to do this?"

"Are we?" Ruby replied. She knew Ward had known her long enough to understand that this meant yes.

♦

It began with a kind of growling, a low drone, which became a vehicle on rolling hills. Dust flew up in its wake, and then Ruby was there, standing behind a jeep as it drove away. "Fuckin'—" somebody called, but she heard only a slice of the word, her mind filling in the rest on its own.

She woke. Someone was yelling. It was the middle of the night in their quiet townhouse complex, and a man's voice was yelling. She couldn't make out the words. She could only lie stiffly, afraid to rustle the sheets. Ward slept on beside her, his palm cupped under his cheek, his mouth ajar. A sound like cars passing through a far-away tunnel wisped from the space between his lips.

"Hey," came the voice. Closer now, and laced with the echoes of the empty street. Footsteps, erratic.

"Hey!" The word rang hard in the stillness, like a bird hitting glass. Ruby sat partway up and smeared the sleep from her eyes.

The curtains were sheer. There was nothing there, but she could picture the man right outside her window, tangled up in the junipers. She imagined the face as one she knew. She'd seen him at the market that morning, dropping new potatoes, one by one, into a plastic bag. She'd recognized his face—the strong eyebrows and round doe eyes—but she hadn't been able to place him. When he'd turned toward her, the way his eyes darted away from hers revealed that he'd recognized her too. They'd walked past each other without another glance. But now, his gaze held fast through the shadows, latching onto hers.

Ruby slid her body back under the covers. Ward did not stir.

In the morning, Ward danced around the kitchen in his usual way, flipping eggs with a spatula in one hand and holding a mug of coffee in the other. Ruby shuffled in, tying her bathrobe belt snug around her waist.

"You slept in," Ward said.

"I was up for a while. Sometime in the night. Like, 3 a.m."

"Really. Why?"

"You slept through it," Ruby said, pouring herself a cup of coffee and sitting at the table. "There was a fight. Some domestic dispute, I think. This guy was yelling and swearing. Fuck this, fuck that. It was so loud. I thought the whole neighbourhood would be up."

"Huh," Ward said. "No kidding. I didn't hear a thing."

"Who do you think it was? Number 9? Remember Helen said her daughter was splitting from her husband and moving in with her for a while?"

"Maybe," Ward said. "Are you sure you didn't dream it?"

"I didn't dream it," she shot back. "I think I know when I'm dreaming and when I'm awake."

"Sheesh, fine." Ward took a seat, setting a plate of eggs and baked beans in front of Ruby and a plate of toast in front of himself. "Over easy. Tell me if they're perfect."

Ruby sliced into the bubble of milky skin, letting the yolk ooze out. "Silky," she said. "Smooth. Yep, perfect." She licked the yolk off the blade of her knife.

"Disgusting," Ward said. He'd always liked his eggs hard, the yolk turned to chalk. "This is your last egg, right?"

"My last egg." She sighed, contemplating the chunk speared on the end of her fork.

"You'd better enjoy it," he said, spreading peanut butter on his wedge of toast. "You've been having a lot of lasts."

"You can't just do this cold turkey," she said. "Cold Tofurky. At least, normal people can't. You've got to ease yourself into it. One step at a time."

"I think I'm starting to feel it already," Ward replied, patting his belly. "More energy, you know? My stomach feels flatter. Fewer rolls."

"That's good." Ruby swirled yolk into her beans, sliding them across her plate. "It's been nine days already. No meat for nine days."

"You're counting? I hadn't even noticed."

She gave him a thin smile, then returned to her eggs. It was better not to respond. She needed time to emerge from the fog of sleep, to adjust to the day. No sense being in a pissy mood. She ate a few more bites and immediately began clearing the dishes.

"I can't believe you didn't wake up," she said, scraping the remnants of her breakfast into the garbage. "It was so loud. Fuck, fuck, fuck. I mean, who does that? Keep it to yourself, for Christ's sake."

◆

Ward's body began to change almost immediately. His upper arms became spindly, the skin white and smooth as birchbark. His calves shaved down to gentle arcs, like a woman's. He seemed thrilled, sneaking glimpses at his figure when he walked past storefront windows. The image of a melting Popsicle stuck in Ruby's mind.

When she was a child, someone—probably her grandmother—had told Ruby that if she didn't eat her protein, her stomach would eat itself from the inside out. She'd believed this for the longest time, even into her adulthood. Whenever her stomach growled, she pictured it as a giant mouth lined with layers of fat, churning, squelching, undulating inside her.

Her body did not shrink. Instead, it seemed to swell. She tried to wear her knee-high leather boots one day, but the zippers would only go halfway up. She wondered if she was allergic to tofu, or if those pepperoni sticks she'd been sneaking from the cafeteria at lunchtime were much fattier than she thought. But she couldn't help it; her body craved them, their smoky flavour, the way her stomach cradled them when she was finished. The last time she'd succumbed to buying one, she tried to picture the cows, their long eyelashes, as she chewed. They were pent up in tiny cells, unable to move. Was pepperoni even made of beef? Or was it pork? She couldn't remember what pigs' eyes looked like.

◆

On their summer vacation last year, Ward and Ruby had taken a road trip through the American Midwest. They'd stopped in South Dakota for Mount Rushmore and marvelled at how distant and tiny the heads looked from the viewing area. Ward had said that great art should look larger in life than it did in photos.

Ruby lingered, walking around to get different angles with her camera, until Ward tugged on her hand and led her back to the parking lot. "Overrated," he said, climbing into the driver's seat. They'd spent only minutes at the site.

The bulk of the day they spent driving through Custer State Park, admiring the towering old-growth pines and moss-coated bridges from inside their car. The clouds travelled overhead, darkening and lightening the atmosphere, as if playing tag with the sun. A storm was imminent, but Ward and Ruby were on vacation. There were things to see.

"Nature," Ward said. "Nothing beats it. It's pure, you know? You learn more about a place from its untouched natural spaces than you ever can from its people."

The sky was sherbet pink when they rolled into Badlands National Park at dusk. It was all prairie grasses and sagebrush— 244,000 acres of it, so the sign said—and, in the distance, cartoonish mountains, like a collection of giant wedding cakes gone wrong, their layers sliding around on melted icing. The tiers of iron-red rock sheets stacked one on top of the other all followed the line of the horizon, so that everything appeared to be a reflection on water, like something out of a Monet painting. The spires that touched the sky were alight.

"They look neon," Ruby remarked, pointing out the window. "Like Disney castles."

"This is incredible," Ward said, his teeth shining pink. "Can you believe there's no one else here?" When they'd entered, they'd seen a couple of cars driving in the other direction, on their way out of the park. Behind them, the dirt road wound its way into the distance, deserted.

"We have this all to ourselves," Ruby said, squeezing Ward's forearm. She felt alive, juiced up on the beauty of the place and the freedom of having no goals, no destination. They were simply existing.

But as the sun's last rays began to fade, Ruby realized there were no street lights. They were in the wilderness on a dirt road, with only the meagre headlights of their 1989 Pontiac lighting the few yards ahead of them. And then it began to rain. What started as fat droplets quickly turned into waterfalls.

"Holy shit," Ward said, slowing the car to a crawl. "Have you ever seen anything like this?"

Ruby hadn't, but she was silent. She hadn't known it was possible for rain to be so heavy that the individual droplets merged to create a solid stream, as though the sky above them was the mouth of a huge tap.

A bolt of purple lightning cracked across the sky, and Ward slammed on the brakes with the shock of it. Ruby could feel the tires slipping on mud as Ward accelerated again. She could see the skin over his knuckles tighten as he gripped the steering wheel with both hands. Thunder, deep and rollicking, reverberated around them. The night had set in. The landscape had disappeared into the black.

"It's just occurred to me," Ruby said quietly. "Maybe we're those naive Canadian tourists that the Americans make fun of. Like, maybe there's a reason we're the only ones here?"

It was Ward's turn not to reply, or perhaps he hadn't heard her over the sound of rain pelting the roof. The car moved forward, but everything was becoming mud. The air all around them was mud, thick curtains of it, with rain sluicing across, sideways, then bouncing off the hood and changing direction so that they could no longer tell where the sky began.

"I can't see a damn thing," Ward said, but he drove on anyway. Ruby wondered if they were even on the road anymore.

Another bolt of lightning lit up the landscape, and then the shroud of darkness seemed to cinch around them like a blindfold.

"What happened?" Ruby said.

"We lost our lights," Ward said. "I think it struck us."

"Oh my god." Ruby checked her hands and arms, as if her veins might be lit up with electricity.

What happened next was spectral in her memory. All she could remember was how the world became pure light for a single instant, and in that instant, Ruby saw a face. It was not a human face. It was wide and flat with stark features, like an African mask. Two dark eyes, shiny as marbles, looked straight through her window, straight at her.

"Holy fuck," Ward said over the rumbling thunder. "Bison."

Bison. Another flash of lightning came right on the heels of the thunder, and Ruby saw now that there was more than one. Bison, dozens of them, flanking their car as it edged forward. In the dark, Ruby could only just make out their silhouettes, like cardboard cut-outs. The bison stood there, frozen in place, watching. It was like driving a hearse in a funeral procession, the bison peering into their car to look upon the deceased one last time. Each time the lightning flashed, Ruby caught another glimpse of a dark moon face, beady eyes set deep in fur. Water dripped from their faces like tears.

When they finally reached the exit gates, Ruby's whole body seemed to dissolve. She realized she had been holding her breath.

"Thank god," Ward said, speeding up as their tires hit the paved road. He had been completely silent for the last half-hour. "That was bonkers. Insane."

"We should have stopped," Ruby said. Her hands were shaking. She held them up for Ward to see.

"We would have gotten stuck," Ward said. "We were sinking in the mud. I couldn't stop."

"I'm so glad you were driving," Ruby said. "I'd have lost my mind."

Looking back, it was one of the times she'd felt most connected to Ward. They had shared that fear. It was something true between them, something that no one else would ever understand.

And yet, Ruby knew that while Ward had been afraid of the mud, the rain, the dark, driving in those conditions—What would have happened if they'd gotten stuck? What if they'd been electrocuted?—those questions hadn't occurred to Ruby. She hadn't been afraid of the weather. She had been afraid of the faces—their baseness, their vacancy. She'd seen them not as animals, but as humans in animal bodies. Like children trapped inside elaborate Halloween costumes. Only the eyes were real.

◆

Her dreams didn't show themselves again for a few weeks. But in the next one, she was attempting suicide. She had been given a poison and careful instructions on how to administer it to herself. First, she had to bite off her thumbnail. It was important that she expose the flesh beneath the nail, open a wound. Then, with the poison held in her mouth, she had to suck her thumb—just the tip—hard. The poison would enter through the thumbnail, she was assured. It would pass through her wound and filter its way through her body to her heart, turning everything black.

But it didn't work, in the end. She didn't do it right. She didn't bite off quite enough of her thumbnail for the poison to enter. She was afraid of the pain. Perhaps she didn't want to die, after all.

Then she got angry at herself, and Ward got angry too. He was yelling at her, fuck this and fuck that. She yelled back at him. Her body began to rise out of the dream, and when her eyes flew open, the yelling was outside her window.

She could hear the man's voice ramping up in intensity, but the words themselves, she could not make out. He was angry, that much was certain. His voice was raw, groping wildly at the same unintelligible sounds over and over again. Ruby wondered if he was even speaking English.

Then, a woman's voice slipped in, brief and frantic. The man cut her off, roaring even louder now. Footsteps smacked across the street, coming toward Ruby's window. She sat up and saw that the window was slightly open.

A shot fired. The sound cracked and ricocheted.

Ruby jumped to her feet. She pulled back the curtain and looked out onto the empty street.

No one. Everything was still.

She looked back at the bed. Ward was turned away from her, on his side. The covers were sandwiched between his legs. The bare skin of his back shone in the moonlight, and his ribs rose and fell in smooth waves.

She climbed back in beside him. "Ward," she whispered, shaking his shoulder. "It's happening again."

Ward lay motionless.

"Ward," she said, this time at full voice. "Ward, get up." She turned him onto his back. He groaned, yanking the duvet over his head.

"Someone's outside," she said. "Listen."

"No one's outside." His muffled voice came through the duvet, but his body lay perfectly still.

"Listen," she said, holding her finger to her lips, poised to hear the voices again. "It was a fucking gun, Ward."

After a few seconds of silence, Ward was softly snoring.

She must have dreamt it, she told herself. But how? She had been awake, wide awake. She had heard the yelling. What if someone had been shot? What else could that sound have been? Had she become one of those people who stand by silently while their neighbour is being brutally murdered? On the news, everyone would ask, *Why didn't someone call the police? Didn't they hear the gunshot? How could they just ignore it?*

Between the crack in the curtains, two dark eyes superimposed over the blank night sky held steady as planets. Whether they were real or imagined seemed impossible to tell. Ruby lay in bed for a long while, listening, but there was nothing. She couldn't think what else to do but wait. She watched Ward's breathing and counted his inhalations. Sleep for him was always unbroken, simple. He was either asleep or awake. Ruby, on the other hand, always seemed to be in between.

◆

"Remember when we saw those bison?" Ruby said as Ward undressed. She lay in bed, watching him. Ward's pants slipped to the floor with the weight of his belt, and his white legs shone. Ruby imagined them as bone, solid bone, no flesh left.

"What are you talking about?" Ward said.

"The bison. You know, the ones in South Dakota? In that badlands park?"

"Oh," he said, peeling off his socks. "Yeah. That was funny." He pulled his shirt over his head, his skin sliding over his ribs.

Ruby didn't reply. She didn't say, *Actually, it was terrifying.* She didn't say, *Somehow, you can let go of everything.* She didn't say, *If you ever thought about your life, you'd picture it like that. Empty.*

For a moment, Ward stood facing her in his briefs. He was spot-lit from above, the halogen track lights pointing down on him, the only light in the room. His eyes were dark sockets. Now she could see the whole of him, see his body in this new light. His limbs like the plastic limbs of a Barbie doll. As if someone popped off his old ones to exchange them for new ones. He flicked off the light.

"They looked sad," Ruby said into the dark. She closed her eyes and sank her head into the pillow.

"What?" Ward climbed in beside her. He shimmied himself under the covers.

"The bison. They looked sad."

"Don't be ridiculous," he said. "They have nothing to be sad about. Nothing at all."

Zora, in the Whirl

I.

I SIT ON MY BUM IN THE GRAVEL, knees bent and legs spread. It's hot and dusty, a haze in the air that makes the tire swing blurry as it creaks and sways back and forth. I can smell the gravel, even taste its tinny flavour all over my tongue. I lean back on the palms of my hands and grind my sandalled feet down, burying my toes. My legs below the knees dusted in chalky white. The dust fills the cracks of my palms, making them look callused and wrinkly—ape hands. Hands like the old bag lady who collects bottles and cans from the trash bins in Fish Creek Park. My spit lands like mud between my legs.

"What are you doing?" Zora trots up, kicking gravel into my shins.

"Spitting." I hold loose strands of hair out of the way, against my ears.

"It's like a little mud bath. We should put ants in it." Zora gets down on her hands and knees and crawls in front of me, her fingers clawing between my feet. She leans forward, jutting her chin out between my bare knees, and spits into the wet spot. "Come on, let's fill the mud bath." She spits again and again: *pit-hoo, pit-hoo, pit-hoo*. Her spit just soaks into the gravel. She sits back on her feet. Her blond hair shines white in the sun.

2.

We dress up in tube tops. Zora stuffs hers with sock balls.

"You have to rub them," Zora says, "and tell me how beautiful I am."

I have agreed to be the boy this time, but in truth we are both pretending to be Zora. Zora, all grown up, her long blond hair and porcelain skin transferred onto a statuesque woman's body. She *is* beautiful, we both believe it, but being told is part of the game.

I close my eyes and gently cup her sock-ball breasts. "Oh Cassandra," I moan. "You're so beautiful." Straddling her waist, I bend to press my lips into her neck, the bridge of my nose brushing her jawline. Sunlight from the open window illuminates the tiny hairs on her skin. A tingly heat, like being on the verge of a sneeze, runs through my body.

"Now the boy kisses the girl," Zora whispers.

"Not on the lips," I say, sitting up.

"No, silly. On the neck, right there. Where you were."

Knowing I cannot say no to Zora, I peck her on the collarbone, then sit back up.

"Okay," she says, pushing me to the side. "Now my turn to be on top of you."

I roll beneath her and she sits on my pelvis.

"The girl needs to sit right here," she says, adjusting her sock balls. "You know why?"

"Yeah," I say, not wanting her to say.

"No, you don't," she insists. "She has to sit here because it's right on top of the penis, that's why." She giggles gleefully. "What?" she says, grinning at my red face. "What's wrong with a PEE-nis, Jenny?"

"Ew," is all I can say.

Zora bounces up and down on my waist, yelling "PEE-nis! PEE-nis! PEE-nis!" and I laugh at first, until the bouncing becomes slower and we both stop smiling and I can feel a bone pressing slightly into the flesh below my belly button.

That's when we hear the door swing open and Zora's mom singing, "Lunchtime, girls!" Zora scrambles off me, tossing the sock balls into her open dresser drawer.

We both kneel on the bed, looking at her mom for a moment as the mattress settles, gauging her expression at finding us here. She only smiles.

"Well?" she says. "Are you hungry?"

Zora jumps off the bed and runs through the door. I follow, my face burning. *She didn't see anything*, I tell myself as I bound down the stairs. *We were jumping on the bed, that's all. We weren't doing anything.*

It's macaroni and cheese, of course, Zora's favourite. Her mom always makes it extra cheesy. When we get down to the kitchen she has a slice of processed cheese already out of its wrapper, and she asks me to break it into little pieces like I do when I feed bread to the ducks. Usually Zora gets this job, but she doesn't seem to care that her mom asked me instead. She stands behind me and watches, not saying a word. Tossing each little piece of cheese into the pot while Zora's mom swirls them in with a wooden spoon makes things feel back to normal. The noodles squelch around in the pot. The little chunks melt into the cheesy goo.

"Yum," Zora says quietly, peering into the pot.

"Somebody's hungry," her mom says, patting Zora on the head. "You girls must have been busy today." When she smiles, her nostrils flare, and her eyes narrow into slits. She has a lot more wrinkles on her face than my mom, and you can see patches of her scalp through her wiry brown hair. After she dishes out two bowls of macaroni she sits at the table holding her elbows and watches us eat.

Like always, Zora gets an orange ring around her mouth where her tongue keeps circling around and around. Sometimes the sauce even dries there like a halo, and tiny cracks worm their way through the coating as she talks and smiles.

While we eat, I have to keep pulling up my tube top, and I get a bit of sauce on it. I dab it with my finger and lick it off. Zora's mom just sits there, watching us. Zora doesn't seem to notice that her tube top has slipped down so that her nipples are peeking out.

"Jenny," her mom says brightly, "these shirts belong to your mother?" Her finger waves at Zora's top.

"No," I say. "They're mine."

"Do you know where she got them?"

I shake my head, licking my spoon.

"Well," she says. "They're pretty slutty."

It's a word I've heard before but don't know. "Thank you," I say.

She flashes a smile.

"I can ask my mom," I say.

Zora's mom squints. "No, it's okay, honey."

Zora brings her empty bowl to her face and licks out the leftover cheese. She has an orange spot on her nose when she puts her bowl down.

"Oh, Zora." Her mom says her name like a yawn and rolls the *r* in her throat: *Zohrr-ra.* "Messy, messy." She leans over and wipes her hand across Zora's face, gathering the cheese between her fingers, and then washes her hands at the sink.

3.

Instead of eating their Easter eggs, Zora's family displays them on the mantel above the fireplace. Each egg sits on its own little wooden stand. It's been weeks and weeks since Easter, but the eggs are still there.

"*You* made these?" I ask when Zora picks one off its stand and puts it in my hand. I cage my fingers around it at first, but open my palm when I feel how light it is. Its hollowness is a kind of magic. An intricate pattern of red and yellow flowers, leafy vines, and repeating diamonds covers the entire shell. It's so perfect, it looks like a computer did it.

"Yeah," Zora says. "My mom helped me a little bit. She showed me how."

I cradle the egg as I transfer it back to Zora's hands. My sister once told me that chinchillas have hollow bones, and that's what I think of, a baby chinchilla. "How did you get all the stuff out?" I ask.

"You poke a hole in it," Zora explains, twisting her pointer finger, "and you blow it out, like this." She puts her lips against the egg's end and puffs her cheeks. "It's really hard not to crack the egg."

I imagine Zora blowing into the egg like she's playing a trumpet, cheeks puffed, face strained and red. I imagine the egg cracking against Zora's lips, yellow jelly flecked with eggshell hanging in syrupy strands from her face.

"Not all of them are hollow," Zora says, taking another egg from the mantel. "See?"

I only get a quick glimpse of the egg before it falls to the floor with a sharp crack.

Zora looks up at me, eyes wide. "You were supposed to take it," she says.

The insides aren't yellow, like I expected. They are greenish grey, the colour of the lake by my grandma's cabin.

When the smell hits our noses, we run. Out the back door, the screen door slamming behind us, down the path between the gnarly rose bushes, and out the back gate to the park, our refuge. We pretend it didn't happen. After a while my mom comes out to tell me that dinner is ready, and when I get up onto our deck I can see Zora still lingering at the park, turning slowly on the tire swing and looking down through its centre at her dangling feet.

We never speak of it again. The next time I'm at Zora's house, the eggs are still sitting in their neat row on the mantel, the empty stand in the centre. The carpet is clean. Not even a ghostly stain to represent the tremendous smell of rot, a smell that had singed the hairs in my nose, filled my head, made my eyes water.

4.

When my eldest sister, Sarah, goes away to horse camp, Zora takes over as her substitute. I hear my mom telling Zora's mom over the phone that it's no trouble at all, she's so used to having three girls around anyway. Zora's mom agrees to let her sleep over at my house every night that week, but insists that she has to go home for dinner when her dad will be there. I've only seen Zora's dad once, never having been invited to stay for dinner. He came home early that day, and when he opened the front door, Zora ran up the stairs. Zora's mom said I should be going then, and on my way out, Zora's dad shook my hand and said he was pleased to meet the famous Jenny. He had a brown moustache like a push broom and smelled like menthol cigarettes. He seems the opposite of my dad, who is baby faced and gentle as a fawn, which makes me feel superior to Zora in one tiny way.

On Thursday, my dad parks the car in the driveway instead of the garage when he gets home from work. Leah and I know what that means.

"Car wash!" we both yell, jumping up from our game of Sorry!

Zora stays sitting on the floor and scrunches up her nose.

"Dad's taking us to the car wash," Leah explains to her.

"Oh," says Zora, twirling her game piece.

"Don't you know what a car wash is?" Leah asks. She's made it her goal this week to assert her role as temporary eldest sister.

"Yeah," says Zora. "I know what it is. I just don't get what's the big deal."

The car wash is an event for me and my sisters. It's the only thing we do with just our dad, no mom allowed. Leah usually sits next to me in the back, leaning forward and poking her head through the opening between the front seats so she can hear Sarah's twenty questions over the *whisshhhhhing* of the car wash. *Is it bigger than a house? No. Is it alive? Yes. Is it an animal? No.* Their voices washed over.

This time, Zora takes the seat beside me as honorary second sister, and Leah takes the front. When we arrive at the gas station, Dad passes the wash ticket to Leah so she can read the numbers to him when he has to punch in the code. I grin at Zora, but she turns to the window, and her chin crumples like she's just sucked on a lemon.

"Here we go!" Dad says when the garage door reels open.

Steam billows out, and water curtains off the rising door. To me, it feels like a spy mission: we've cracked the code to the secret bunker and now we're sneaking in, inch by inch, looking from side to side as though a monster is going to pop out any second. Then, the spinning washers emerge from the shadows: eight-foot-tall girl-eating yetis, their eyes, mouths, and noses hidden behind veils of bristly blue shag. Their limbless bodies flank the car in perfect formation, silent, unmoving, waiting for the right moment to attack. Our car keeps edging in, Dad tapping the gas, and the only sound I can hear is the dripping of water from the yetis' bodies. I imagine it's drool dribbling from their mouths and soaking into their beards, *drip-dripping* onto the cement floors. As soon as Dad parks the car, my heart starts to beat so fast I can feel it thumping in my ears.

But then, all at once, the yetis begin to spin, and they aren't vicious at all—they only want to dance. Their thick hairs flare out everywhere like a hundred hula skirts stacked on top of each other. They twirl against the car, begging it to join the dance, and whip trails of froth back and forth like ribbons. The hairs *thwick* rhythmically past my window, bubbles swirling on the glass.

It feels to me like a dream.

I sit quietly, watching with my hands in my lap, the way my mom taught me to do in the audience at the ballet. I imagine the blue hairs flicking across my face, over my arms and body, drenching my skin with warm, soapy water.

I don't even notice Zora's whimpering until Dad is driving through the exit door, looking over his shoulder, saying "What's wrong? What's wrong?" Zora's face is splotched with red, her cheeks wet with tears. A coating of snot glistens on her upper lip.

I don't know what to say or do, so I just sit and watch. I watch while Dad parks the car and takes Zora to the gas station bathroom. In the time that they are gone, Leah and I are quiet, and I pick at the grey spot on the upholstery where I once accidentally smeared some bubble gum.

"What a baby," Leah says under her breath when she sees them coming out a few minutes later. Zora is smiling, holding Mars bars for all of us.

After Zora goes home for dinner that evening, my mom tells me not to ask Zora why she cried, not to talk about it at all with her or Leah. From the way my mom's voice sounds, I know I shouldn't ask why. I'm sure, anyway, that Zora was just scared of the yetis and that asking her would be embarrassing for us both. After all, we are good at pretending, and I know we will go back to playing after dinner as though nothing happened and build our blanket fort in the dining room and crawl inside and zip our sleeping bags together at bedtime. But Zora doesn't return that night after dinner. She doesn't sleep over again. She comes over to my house to play a couple more times, then she moves away.

◆

Years later, I see Zora at the mall, standing in line to buy a frozen yogourt. I am seventeen, and so is she. Her long hair is now a dirtier blond, and it's braided in tight cornrows across her skull. She is short, maybe five feet. Besides her hair and the black eyeliner that rims her eyes, she is a magnified version of her child self. Puberty doesn't appear to have altered her quite yet; her limbs are still skinny, her chest nearly flat. Her skin is still pure white and perfect, her eyes a striking ice blue, even from a distance.

For a brief moment, I think about approaching her, but I quickly realize that would be impossible. What is there to say? *Hi, do you remember me? I remember you ...* Our history doesn't seem real anymore, as though it belongs to another world. Now, from my height, I would look down on her. I would be able to see the top of her head, rivers of scalp between the braids.

At the food court, I meet my boyfriend, Wayde, and our friend Jolene. Wayde is growing a mousy moustache.

"Have you encouraged this?" Jolene asks, pointing at the moustache.

I give Wayde a peck on the lips. "It's like kissing a kiwi," I say to Jolene. She laughs, her teeth flashing like lights against her black-lipsticked mouth.

Wayde rolls his eyes. "It's only been three days," he says, combing his upper lip with the side of his finger. I can tell by the stony look on his face that he's upset again. He's quiet as the three of us share some New York Fries, Jolene and I complaining about Bio and making plans for Halloween and mocking the Rubik's Cube guy who showboats at the food court every Saturday. I'm relieved when we get into our seats at the movie theatre and no one has to talk anymore.

It's not until after the movie, when we've parted ways with Jolene and gotten back to Wayde's house, that he finally says something.

"You know, you're kind of a bitch when Jolene's around," he says.

"Is that a problem?" I say, feigning apathy.

"All you guys do is make fun of people," he says. "As if you're better than everyone else."

I shrug. "Maybe we are."

"She's a fucking dog," Wayde says. "With that nose ring? She thinks she's all edgy and mysterious, but no one thinks she's hot. At least you've got tits." He pushes me down on his bed and slides his hands up my shirt. His fingers claw at my breasts.

"Ow," I say, pulling away. "What are you doing, making meatballs?"

"Fuck you," Wayde says. "Why don't you just go fuck Jolene already?"

"Why? You wanna watch?" I unzip my jeans and slip them off with my underwear.

Wayde stares at me for a moment. "What is the matter with you?" he says. Then his face softens and he unzips his own pants.

A few weeks earlier, for our six-month anniversary, he gave me a book on the Kama Sutra. "I think we need to spice up our sex life," he said, which struck me as such a contrived thing to say, especially for a seventeen-year-old, that I couldn't help but cringe. But I took the book graciously anyway, and we flipped through the pages together, dog-earing the ones we agreed to try. On one page, there was a photo of a naked woman lying on the floor, arms raised and palms turned up, ready to receive a man who was standing over her backward, pointing his bare, shiny butt in her face. It might have been a botched Photoshop job, or maybe the print quality was poor, but the woman's skin was an unsettling manila-yellow colour, and so smooth and unblemished that it looked painted. Her expression seemed to belong to someone lying in the grass on a summer's day, lazy and detached, absently musing on the shapes of the clouds. "That looks cool," Wayde said, folding over the corner of the page. I didn't want to tell him that I couldn't understand the logistics of the position. After we looked at the book together, I hid it under a pile of sweaters in my closet and never looked at it again.

Wayde hasn't brought it up since then. We have sex the way he usually likes it, with him on top. I think about whether Wayde would be attracted to Zora. Would she ask him to kiss her on the neck and tell her she's beautiful? I see her as the woman lying on the floor, arms raised to Wayde, the same vacant expression on her face, except her skin is white and soft, as I remember it. Then I stop myself; I open my eyes and look at Wayde, at his bony chest heaving above me, his face scrunched and straining, the little hairs of his moustache lifting ever so slightly with the curl of his upper lip, like tiny searching antennae. A strand of spit falls from the corner of his mouth and lands on the bridge of my nose, then dribbles into my eye socket. I turn my head and wipe it against the pillow before he notices.

When we're done, Wayde turns on the TV, and our spat has dissolved. I say I have to get home for dinner, and he watches the screen while I get dressed. This is our pattern now; offering him sex is a lot easier than mustering defences against his accusations. He gets me to wrap up the used condom in a wad of toilet paper and stuff it in my pocket to throw in the garbage can at the bus stop so his mom won't find it. When I get home, I change all of my clothes.

At dinner that night, I tell my mom and my sisters about seeing Zora.

"Oh?" my mom says. "Did she look the same?"

"Pretty much," I say. "She had these weird braids. And she's little. Like, way shorter than me."

"Really?" says Sarah. "I always saw her becoming a model or something."

Leah snorts. "You weren't there when she stayed with us that summer. Something was not right about her."

"What?" I say, balking. "What do you mean?"

"Well, for one thing, she was a compulsive liar."

I look at my mom. She doesn't move to dispute this. She's putting green beans on her plate, listening.

"What did she lie about?" I ask. "I don't remember that at all."

"All kinds of things," Leah goes on. "You know, like she could do twenty cartwheels in a row and she had three boyfriends and her uncle was a spy ... I don't remember all of it." I realize now that these details had been facts to me. As a kid, I'd never questioned their truthfulness.

"I'm just glad she moved away," my mom chimes in, "and that the two of you just drifted naturally after that. I didn't have to intervene."

"Intervene in what?" I say. My heart is suddenly pumping fast. An image of Zora straddling me, that same tingly feeling. I recognize it now as shame.

"I guess you were too young to understand," Mom says. She hesitates for a moment. "I wasn't keen on you two being so close. I don't know the details, but her home life was not good. She once told your dad that her father molested her or something." Mom swats at the air with her free hand, a gesture that suggests this comment should be dismissed.

Forks clink against plates. I look at my sisters' faces pointed down at their food and realize I'm the only one who is shocked. Shocked that Zora might have been molested, but even more shocked by Mom's callousness.

"That's sad," says Sarah. In the silence that follows, I wonder what Sarah means by sad. Sad that it had happened to Zora, or sad that she claimed it had happened?

"More beans, anyone?" asks Mom. It's clear that she means this to be the end of the conversation. We've learned not to talk about problems with fathers. Mom divorced our dad when we were younger, which was a surprise to everyone but her, and we, her girls, naturally became her steadfast allies. We know better than to ask questions. Just like Zora and I practised that summer, we've become good at pretending.

5.

"Spinny!" Zora shrieks, pulling the tire swing as she runs in tight circles.

I grip the chains and tuck in my legs as I spin in circle after circle. Zora lets go and stands, panting. She keeps me spinning, swiping the tire's treaded side to propel it along on its course. I try to focus on all the images whirling past: a brown fence, a bike rider on the path, the slide shimmering silver in the sunlight, the horses, Zora, a pine tree, houses, the fence, two people walking a dog, the slide, the horses, Zora.

"Around the world!" Zora catches the tire and pushes it in a wide arc over her head, her feet skittering in the gravel. She ducks under the tire's rotation, her head just narrowly missing the swoop of my dangling feet. In the whirl, I see Zora smoothing down her tangled hair and then walking toward the horses, a cloud of gravel dust trailing behind her.

I lean back and stick my legs out. The swing slows. The sun hangs low in the sky, and when I look down at the ground, I see the gravel flecked with shadows, lit orange by late-afternoon light, and my own long shadow sweeping across it like a noiseless, soaring bat.

Kids in Kindergarten

SHE SAID THE ONES WHOSE MOTHERS didn't really want them were always the best behaved.

"They'll do anything to please you," Rebecca said, stirring her virgin Caesar with a spear of pickled asparagus.

I looked at the carcass of a fly lying at the edge of the bar top. All that was left was a shrivelled peppercorn with wings sticking out of it.

"There's this one kid, Lonnie. Has a little blond rat-tail. He asks me every single day if I want some of his candy bar, just because one time I told the class I was craving chocolate and he offered half of his KitKat, which I took. I'd gone on about how kind and generous he was, and his eyes were just like stars."

"He has a candy bar every day?" I said.

"I know." Rebecca rolled her eyes. "Some parents. I tell ya, this kid's not getting any sugar until he's at least two." She patted her belly as if to alert the fetus to her vow.

Rebecca had only recently begun to show, even though she was now six months along. Her bump was a perfect ball of dough over which a cotton dress was stretched. Last time I had seen her, she'd worried aloud about how long it would be before her belly button popped out. "Don't you think it looks gross when you can see it poking out under someone's shirt like a huge zit?" she'd said.

"So, is he bright, then? Lonnie?" I asked her.

"Mm," she said, swallowing a gulp of her drink. "Not in the least. Can't even count to five. But I feel like his emotional intelligence is higher than most adults.'"

"Adversity builds character," I said.

"Exactly. I mean, you can't really blame the mother. She's got two older boys also, twins. Clearly Lonnie was an accident."

An accident. I bobbed my head in agreement, listening to her anecdotes about the various kids in her class—kids on behavioural meds, kids with puppet phobias, kids who licked their lips raw, kids with designer knapsacks. Really, I was thinking about how I'd spent more than a decade of my youth desperately avoiding an "accident." When I lost my virginity to my boyfriend at sixteen, he'd broken down into tears after coming inside me because we hadn't used a condom. "How could I be so fucking stupid?" he'd said, both of us watching his dripping penis slowly deflate. Even though I'd taken the bus to the clinic that same evening for a morning-after pill, for weeks I was convinced that it was over, I'd been implanted, and now a tiny nugget was growing inside of me, sprouting arms and legs and fingernails and hair soft as feathers. I grew up as all girls did, believing that without some form of birth control, getting pregnant was inevitable penance for the sin of having sex. Then, once we'd grown up enough for a baby to be acceptable, we believed that it would happen when we commanded it, like pushing a button on a microwave.

It had for Rebecca. While Greg and Claudia had slid into their roles as devoted spouses, swapping recipes for antioxidant-rich meals to cook for us and expounding on the fertility benefits of replacing coffee with yerba maté, Rebecca and I planned out how we could get pregnant at the same time, determining that she should go off the pill a few months before the day of my IVF, since it might take some time for her body to adjust. But she'd gotten pregnant immediately. She'd texted me a photo of her and Greg holding up a positive pregnancy test with the caption, *Turns out we're super fertile!* Now, their first child, Harriet, was already three years old.

The server came by to take our orders. Rebecca did not seem to notice when I asked for a ginger ale instead of wine. She was examining the nails of her left hand, which were painted an assortment of colours like Chiclets.

"Anyway," she said, once the server had left, "not to scare you about them or anything. They're going to love you. I just want you to be prepared."

"I'm excited for it," I said. "I love reading aloud." I took a sip of my drink. "This ginger ale tastes a bit funny," I muttered, though it didn't. I'd thought that ordering a virgin drink would be enough to get Rebecca to ask. The last time she'd asked was over a year ago. But then it occurred to me that if she did ask, I wouldn't know how to tell her.

I quickly redirected. "If I'm boring, you'll have to give me a signal."

"A signal," she repeated. "Like this?" She did the shocker, grinning.

"Yes," I said. "That'll work."

◆

When I got home after dinner, Claudia was back. She'd taken the red-eye from Shanghai and was indeed red eyed, but I couldn't tell if it was from exhaustion or from crying. Maybe both.

"You didn't have to come," I said. I'd expected myself to break down when I saw her, but I felt wrung out.

"Of course I came," she said, wrapping me up in her arms. "I just wish I could've gotten here sooner. The one time I miss my connection …"

"It's not your fault," I said, pulling away. I didn't know why, but I felt annoyed.

"Honey," she said, turning up her palms. "I'm so sorry. How do you feel? Is there any pain?"

"Not anymore," I said. "It was quick."

"And have you been to the doctor yet?"

"No," I said. "I'm going tomorrow to drop off the sample."

Claudia pressed a hand to her mouth. "I'm going with you," she said.

"No, it's fine," I said. "I have to go to Rebecca's school straight afterward anyway. I'm doing the guest reading for her class at nine-thirty."

"You're still doing that?"

"Yeah. Why not?"

"I'm sure Rebecca would understand if you had to cancel. Or postpone."

"It's fine," I said.

Claudia bit her nail. I went to the kitchen and put the kettle on to boil.

"Where is it?" she said eventually.

"What?"

"The ... sample."

"In the fridge."

"You put it in the fridge?"

"That's where you're supposed to put it," I said. "You have to keep it fresh."

Claudia shut her eyes. "Okay, I just—I don't want to see it. Is that horrible?"

"No," I said. *Yes*, I thought. "I'll put it in a bag or something."

"I'm sorry," she said.

I didn't say that I hadn't wanted to see it either. I didn't say that I'd expected it to look like a baby, like it had in the ultrasound, with a bulbous head and little frog arms waving, but that it came out instead as a purplish-red sac, like a chicken liver. I'd held it in a wad of tissues because I couldn't bear to touch it and dropped it into a mason jar. A faded label for spiced peaches was still stuck to the side.

After I concealed the jar in a crumpled paper bag, Claudia and I snuggled up on the couch together with our tea, and she stroked my hair. I didn't know how to tell her that it wasn't soothing—it felt like being raked taut and snapped like old gum. I felt as though I were different now; something inside my body had shifted, and now every organ and muscle and bone had clicked into a new position. Even my eyeballs, which now seemed to focus on new shapes—the insides of things rather than the outsides, the blank spaces in between.

"This is good," Claudia whispered. "This time, we'll get some answers."

♦

I knew which one Lonnie was as soon as I walked in. The rat-tail was a giveaway, but so were his strange wide eyes, which made him look older than the other kids, even though he was about half their size. He was colouring a photocopy of a jack-o'-lantern, carefully filling the eye holes with pink marker. He had a small round nose and a slight mouth, and he held himself in a similarly diminutive way, all of which made him look like a field mouse sniffing about in a world that was far too big for him.

Rebecca seemed to take on a different persona in her role as teacher. Her nature wasn't ordinarily maternal or particularly warm, even with her own daughter. But here, in her classroom, Rebecca was Maria von Trapp, announcing storytime with a song she sang to the tune of "If You're Happy and You Know It."

"If you're ready for a story clap your hands!" *Clap, clap*. Her voice was pristine as glass, her smile painted a candy pink.

The kids sprang from their seats, skipping over to the circular rainbow rug in the corner of the classroom and cannonballing into what were obviously their habitual spots. Some of the girls sang along to the song. A boy with a mop of black hair groaned and threw his head back, clapping his hand on his forehead, one eye gauging my reaction, which I was sure to conceal. Lonnie rose from his seat, lifting his eyes from his paper as though waking from a dream, and walked over with measured steps, sliding his hands into the pockets of his grey sweatpants. He kept them tucked in as he dropped into a cross-legged position near the outer edge of the rug, behind a gaggle of girls who were arranging themselves to braid each other's hair.

"I'm so happy to be here," I said to the kids, hating how flat my voice sounded in contrast to Rebecca's chirpy teacher tone. Back when Rebecca had asked me to be a guest reader for her class, I'd assumed she'd recognized my natural, even instinctual way with kids, until I discovered she'd been asking everyone she knew. I'd agreed immediately, certain that the visit would confirm to everyone, especially myself, how deserving I was of motherhood. But now, I felt the urge to perform. "I'm going to read one of my favourite books of all time," I went on, honeying my voice, amplifying its hills and valleys. "*The Magic Finger.*"

"How special!" said Rebecca. "So, boys and girls, let's put on our best listening ears for our friend." She tugged her earlobes and the children mimicked her.

I only got about halfway through the book before the kids began fidgeting. One of them splayed out onto his belly like a seal and started rocking himself from side to side on his hands. Another had taken off her shoes and was flicking little lint balls she'd picked from the rug into them. Rebecca seemed embarrassed and a few times gestured at the disrupters to stop, but I didn't actually care. I wasn't reading to them; I was reading to Lonnie. He was still the entire time, listening, watching me with those round eyes. Watching *me*, not even looking at the pictures that I displayed face out, panning the book across the audience. He had a far-off look on his face, his eyes practically shimmering, and I knew he was imagining himself as the character in the story—what it would be like to have his own magic finger with the power to punish those who were cruel and selfish, those who didn't deserve their perfect, cushy lives.

"All right, boys and girls," Rebecca interrupted, just as I was about to turn a page. "I think it might be time for a little break." She broke into song once again. "Recess, everybody out! Recess, 'cause it's time to run and shout!"

Rebecca and I put on our shoes along with the kids, and she explained that it was a longer story than the kids were used to. Over her white dress, she put on a long red peacoat she could no longer button all the way, so her belly stuck out from the folds like it was peeking from a curtained stage.

"Sorry," I said. "I'm clearly out of touch with kids."

"Oh, please," she said, "You can't help it. We'll give them fifteen to blow off steam and then we'll see how they are."

I wanted to leave. It was obvious that storytime would not resume when recess was over. But I stood with Rebecca, our breath puffing into vapour, watching the kids leap and swing and skid in the gravel.

Rebecca clucked her tongue. "Oh, Ashton," she said, spying some confrontation off to the side of the playground. "The little shit. He's one of the ones I told you about. The one whose parents treat him like a little emperor."

It was the mop-haired kid, and he was standing on the basketball court at the edge of huge puddle. On the other side of the puddle stood Lonnie, his chin pointed down, his eyes, stricken with suspicion, aimed up at Ashton's. With a careless swipe of his booted foot, Ashton sloshed muddy water in Lonnie's direction. Lonnie's grey sweatpants turned black up to the knees, and he raised his arms, shocked, winded.

Rebecca ran over. "Ashton!" she said. She grabbed his arm, and a half-eaten KitKat dropped from his hand into the dirt. "That is *not* how we treat our friends, is it? I'm going to have to call your parents again." She turned to Lonnie. "Are you all right?"

He nodded, still holding up his arms like wings.

"Okay, boys and girls!" Rebecca hollered. "Back inside!"

Lonnie's sweatpants had wicked the muddy water up to the thighs by the time he reached the doors to the school. He went ahead while Rebecca held open the doors for the kids, a few filing in at a time. I followed Lonnie, who moved quickly into the classroom. He went directly to a cupboard behind Rebecca's desk and retrieved a pair of green slacks before disappearing into the bathroom. He emerged within moments, holding his balled-up pants in two hands. The green slacks hung loosely from his hips. Rebecca was still in the hall, swept up in a flurry of kids tossing off jackets and boots.

"Here," I said to Lonnie. I found an old grocery bag in my purse and took the ball from his hands. A wet pantleg flopped out as I dropped the ball into the bag. I tied it up, passing it back to Lonnie.

By the time Rebecca came back into the classroom, Lonnie was sitting at his desk with his hands folded, his knees pressed tightly under the desk in the ill-fitting slacks.

"Sorry for cutting you short," Rebecca said to me. "Maybe we can try again sometime?"

She'd already forgotten about Lonnie. I knew that after I'd left, she and the kids would go on with their day as usual. They'd all forget, except Lonnie, who would keep feeling the cold splash of the water hitting him over and over, the shapeless wet crawling up his legs.

Ashton was just coming in the door as I went out. He tried to brush past me, but I stood in the way.

He looked up at me, incredulous. I stared back.

"Everything okay, Ashton?" Rebecca called.

I bent down to his level and whispered in his ear. "You're a waste," I said. "A filthy waste."

◆

I would never see Rebecca again. Ashton's parents would complain to the principal, and in the end, neither of us would be able to find a way to forgive the other. She would name her son Roger, after her dad. And mine—this one, for whom I'd made another womb in the bottom of my purse, nestled in my wool scarf—mine would have a name with the sound of a stone, a thing with no face, and without memory.

Butter Buns

GAVIN'S MOTHER HUNG THE POSTER of Arnold Schwarzenegger flexing his biceps in what she called her "weight room"—a spare room in the basement packed with the family's unwanted or rarely used things. Arnie, in the prime of his youth, posed in the coy, hip-cocked manner of pro bodybuilders, his muscles tanned and oiled. The muscles reminded Gavin of the butter buns they always had on the table at Thanksgiving, clumped together with their shiny egg-washed tops peeking from the bowl. He teased his mother whenever she retreated to the room to lift weights. "Going to spend some quality time with Butter Buns?" he would say, or "Say hi to Butter Buns for me."

"It's motivation," she once said in retort. "He was pretty amazing in his day, you know. He could deadlift 710 pounds. Imagine."

"But he looks subhuman," Gavin said. "I mean, there is such a thing as too much muscle." In truth, the poster creeped him out, especially when he was forced to go into the room to get his skis or camping gear from the storage closet and Arnie's lumpy silhouette leered at him in the dark like some kind of mythical beast.

"What about me?" she said, flexing her own biceps. "Too much?"

"Well," he said, "it's weird having a mom who's ripped. I'll say that much." What he meant by *ripped* was more muscular than himself. She didn't know, of course, that his friends referred to her as "the MILF" whenever she came up in conversation. Their own mothers were suitably plump, soft as dough around the middle, flaunting their cellulite-riddled thighs at the public pool—the way Gavin's mother had used to be. Then, a couple of years ago, when Gavin was just starting high school, she suddenly hired a personal trainer and started buying value-sized drums of protein powder, which she mixed into horridly green smoothies each morning to wash down her four-egg-white omelette. At first she'd wanted him to go to the gym with her and nagged him about it each evening when she was about to leave, but it felt to Gavin like a motherly attempt to combat his lanky teenage insecurity.

"We could do it together," she'd said, knocking him on the shoulder. "Like a mother-son bonding type thing."

"Nah," Gavin said. "I don't like lifting weights. Too repetitive."

"Ha! And swimming laps isn't?"

He shrugged. He worked at the YMCA pool as a lifeguard, but he was reluctant to tell his mother that he hadn't actually kept up a regular swimming routine since he quit the swim club years ago.

"Well," his mother continued, "it's the repetition that I like. It's comforting. I just think about how each time I do a rep, the muscle is getting a tiny bit stronger."

She did get stronger, bit by bit. Her resolve actually impressed Gavin, though he'd never have said it. One day he suddenly noticed the definition of her shoulders, bare except for the straps of her tank top, as she tied her hair back in a ponytail. Her muscles tightened and undulated like animals moving beneath the skin. Eventually, she stopped asking Gavin's father to lift boxes or open jars for her. In fact, she seemed to stop asking Gavin's father anything at all. Gavin remembered coming home from a friend's house on a Saturday night to find his father asleep on the couch, the purring cat nestled in the crook of his arm, and his mother in the kitchen, pulsing her smoothie again and again, struggling to dislodge a big chunk of carrot that had gotten stuck under one of the blades. The harsh, grating sound had become so integrated into their family life that neither his father nor the cat stirred, and it was then that Gavin realized he hadn't seen his parents touch for as long as he could remember. They seemed to be perpetually across the house from each other, as though their bodies were repelled by invisible magnetic forces.

When they finally split, Gavin's mother took the Vitamix, along with her collection of free weights and her Bowflex, to the new house she and Gavin now rented in Mission. The Arnie poster came too, transplanted to a new weight room with white walls and hardwood floors. Everything else, she insisted, was tainted with bad memories.

Some months later, Gavin asked his father why they had decided to get divorced in the end.

"I never really understood the bodybuilding thing," his father said. "At first it was great for her to be so fit, but at a certain point it became kind of … grotesque." Gavin must have blushed at the force of the word, because his father quickly added, "Sorry, that came out wrong. She changed. And not just on the outside. We both did."

♦

In Gavin's Film 100 class, they learned about the Wilhelm scream. It came up in their discussion of *Reservoir Dogs*, a piece of trivia offered by his professor in passing.

"It happens when Mr. Pink knocks over a pedestrian." The professor imitated the shriek for the class. The students laughed. The professor explained how the scream was first recorded in 1951 as a sound effect for a scene in which a man is eaten by an alligator in a film called *Distant Drums*. Then the scream was repurposed in a few other films, which became a kind of running joke among insiders, including the sound designer for *Star Wars*, who used it in a scene where Luke Skywalker shoots a stormtrooper. He incorporated the scream in all of the subsequent Star Wars and Indiana Jones films. The joke took off after that, until eventually the scream had worked its way into hundreds of films over the course of several decades.

What struck Gavin was that the scream was not particularly memorable or passionate. He hadn't noticed it at all when they watched *Reservoir Dogs* in class. In fact, when he went home that evening and looked up a YouTube recording of the scream, he was at first unconvinced that he had found the right sound effect. It was more of a yelp than a scream, with no hint of the horror that being eaten alive by an alligator would entail.

When he met with his professor to discuss his ideas for his term paper, he found himself mentioning the scream. He'd come into the meeting without a clue about his thesis, but when the professor asked what had interested him most in the course, he'd said, like a dope, "Well, the stuff you said about the Wilhelm scream was pretty cool." He immediately regretted sounding so inarticulate, but the professor seemed to perk up.

"Okay," he said, picking up his pen and notepad. "So what is it about *Reservoir Dogs* that you found so interesting? Perhaps you're interested in Tarantino's somewhat comedic treatment of violence?"

"Uh, sure," Gavin said. "Maybe. I just thought what you said about the scream was interesting."

"Ah," said the professor. "It's kind of a fun fact, isn't it?" He turned his pen on its end and tapped it against the desk. "All right, then, what about the Wilhelm scream in the film? What do find so interesting about this moment?"

Gavin knew he couldn't say the truth, because the truth was that he didn't know. The truth was that he hadn't realized until he was packing up his bag after the lecture that day that he'd been captivated. He hadn't even yawned once. And he'd begun thinking about all the films he wanted to watch again so that he could try to pick out the scream.

"I guess," he ventured, "it's something about how it's got a life of its own now. Like, how it's become this thing, this thing in and of itself, and it's been used in all these different films."

The professor laid his pen down on the blank notepad. "Yes," he said. "It's certainly become a kind of cultural artifact of the twentieth century in that regard."

Gavin nodded as though he understood.

"But I don't know that you have a *paper* here," the professor continued. "I don't think it's enough to simply focus on the scream. If you can find a way to make an argument about the role of the scream in the film, you might have something."

Gavin left quickly thereafter, with the empty promise that he would return once he had brainstormed more ideas.

◆

When Gavin learned of the abortion, it had been four years since it happened.

What had started as a casual conversation at White Spot about Gavin never wanting kids of his own turned into his mother admitting that she had wanted more children at one time. Her face then cracked into tears just as Gavin took a giant bite of his burger, leaving him to watch her dribble and sputter into her napkin while he chewed, mayonnaise seeping from the corner of his mouth. His mother spilled the whole story right then and there, apparently unfazed by the scandalized stares of the old couple in the booth across from them. She'd unexpectedly become pregnant when she and Gavin's father were on the brink of separation. She'd wanted to keep the baby at first.

"But your father …" She paused. "He didn't think it was a good idea."

Gavin had seen pictures of aborted fetuses on the billboards that the university pro-life club had paraded around the campus. They were purple and slick with blood, strangely menacing with their fused-shut eyelids and skinny limbs.

"So … do you regret it?" he asked her.

"No," his mother said. "Not at all. It was the right choice."

"Okay," Gavin said, picking at his fries. He didn't know what else to say. He thought about rubbing her back the way she always did for him when he was upset, but then he would have had to slide out from his side of the booth and go over to hers, which seemed like an awkward ordeal, during which the moment would pass.

"Sorry," she said. "I didn't mean to unload this on you."

"It's fine." Gavin thought about how only a few weeks ago, they'd driven past a gang of pro-lifers protesting outside the hospital, and his mother had joked, "Should I go all She-Hulk on those assholes, or what?" It was the first time he'd realized his mother was pro-choice. When she rolled down her window to yell, "My body, my choice!" he felt a pang of proud ownership of her. His cool mom, a raging feminist. He told her then about how the pro-life demonstrators on campus got egged, and together they'd poured scorn on them, laughing like friends.

Now, the woman crying into her Cobb salad seemed to be someone else. She must have seen the confused expression on his face, because she said, "It doesn't just go away. The grief. I know it's been a while now, but …"

Gavin could feel himself squirming. He'd thought he was close with his mother, but they had never talked like this before. He'd never heard her say the word *grief*.

"I'm glad I did it, but making a decision like that still hurts," she said. You don't realize how hard it's going to be until you have to do it. It can be the right decision, but it still feels like a loss."

Gavin reached across the table and patted her hand with his greasy one. He couldn't help but think then, while she gave a little embarrassed smile and wiped away her tears, about his mother's body under her clothes, under her skin. Its insides—veins, nerves, organs, like the diagrams pinned to the wall in the doctor's office. A body like any other woman's, with a space hidden inside her to grow another human. And that space had been his at one time, the only world he had ever known, though it now seemed so entirely and privately hers.

He wondered if she'd seen the fetus after they removed it. And where it had gone afterward. Was it cremated, or thrown in the garbage like a useless lump of flesh? And although he knew that the fetus had been far too small to be noticeable in his mother's belly, he felt as though he should have known, should have some-how seen through the layers of clothing and skin that had obscured the unformed thing inside.

♦

Gavin spent the Saturday after he met with his professor marathon-watching the original Star Wars and Indiana Jones films, searching for the split-second moment where the Wilhelm scream was embed-ded. Each time he caught it, he felt a small thrill and promptly paused the movie to track back and rewatch it a few times over, just to take in how cleverly integrated it was in the scene. Later, he found a YouTube video that compiled various Wilhelm screams from a few dozen of the hundreds of films that had used it. Watching them like that, one after another, burned the sound of the scream into his mind—the ever so slightly raspy shriek of it, which made him pic-ture the inside of a throat, vocal cords vibrating. But the repetition was also oddly etherizing. After the third or fourth time watching the compilation, the noise began to sound mechanical, and Gavin began to see it as just that: a noise, something inanimate, cut loose from the screamer and floating off into empty space.

He knew, however, that this kind of thinking wasn't what his professor had meant by "brainstorming." He did try to sit down with his notebook, rereading the half page of half-hearted notes he'd written on *Reservoir Dogs* and thinking about what the professor had said about the role of the scream. The only conclusion he was able to arrive at was that the scream was really about something bigger than itself. It had the uncanny ability to adapt to its environment; you could place it in any context and it would blend in, invisible to all but those select few who were deliberately searching for it. Was that enough, though, for it to mean anything?

By the day the term paper was due, Gavin had done nothing but scribble the word *invisible* in his notebook.

◆

Classes ended, and Gavin scraped by with a 53 percent in his film class, having failed to submit anything for his term paper. He was relieved that he wouldn't have to see his professor ever again. The professor had seemed so hopeful and spirited about his ideas, and Gavin knew he had been a disappointment. But only a week later, he did see his professor again, this time at the YMCA pool on Gavin's Sunday morning shift. Thankfully, Gavin was surveying the lane swimming at the other end of the facility, where he could go unnoticed. Seeing his professor half-naked, his farmer's tan on full display, made Gavin struggle to recall his first name and, for a moment, wonder whether he even knew it. Dean, he thought it was, such a fitting name for a professor. But here, he was in dad mode, showcasing waterlogged neon-orange shorts, a freckled chest, and a pouchy gut while he coaxed his young son into the wading pool. He'd always looked so pressed and starched at school in his checked dress shirts and blazers, as though he'd run an iron over his whole body, flattening every bump and crease.

Dean was fully absorbed in his son, blind to Gavin watching him. The boy could not have been more than two. He stood on the ramp with his toes touching the water, grinning with glee at his dad, who held his arms out wide. Even though Gavin was too far away to hear, he could tell that Dean was saying, "Swim to Daddy!" in that syrupy tone that parents use for young children. The boy squealed and bent down to splash his hands, sending up little sprinkles of water that showered down and made him squeal all the more. The whole scene was sweet, one of those picture-perfect dad moments that Gavin was sure he had experienced with his own dad at that age.

Later, when Gavin was returning from his break, he ran right into Dean, who was emerging from the bathroom, still dripping, his son on his hip. Gavin tried to turn his head away and pretend not to see him, but Dean waved cheerfully and called his name.

"Oh, hey," Gavin said, feigning surprise. He felt the urge to stay a good distance from Dean's flabby torso, wet and shiny as a sealskin.

"Working here for the summer, are you?" asked Dean, as his son wriggled in his arms. He slung the boy against his chest and hooked his arm between his chubby little legs so that he sat face forward, thrust before Gavin. Without waiting for Gavin to answer, Dean said, "This is Ian. We're starting swimming lessons soon, so we'll probably see you around quite a bit."

"Cool," Gavin said. Realizing then that he was just one among hundreds of students, he wondered if Dean even remembered their conversation in his office.

"Whoa, okay buddy," Dean said, as he juggled the boy. "I promised him we'd go in the waves. Better get in there before it's over!"

Gavin gave the boy a cheesy thumbs-up, thankful that Dean seemed just as keen to keep the exchange brief. Gavin went back to his post at the lanes, losing interest as Dean waded into the wave pool and installed Ian upon a foam floaty shaped like a whale. But only minutes later, a sharp whistle drew Gavin's attention back. The clusters of heads scattered across the wave pool flicked in unison toward the source of the sound: some sort of commotion in the deep end. The waves were going full force, and a group of teenagers—two boys and three girls—were roughhousing with pool noodles, carelessly throwing their weight around like excited puppies, ignorant of the largeness of their bodies. The whistle tweeted once again, then twice more. The teens ignored it, now creating a spectacle as other swimmers glared and dashed away. But there, caught up in the churning water, Gavin spotted the whale floaty, abandoned. A stray foot kicked it hard. The floaty upturned, dipping halfway under the water and then shooting back up, jostled in a flurry of splashing arms and legs. Dean's head poked from the water's surface for just a moment, and Gavin could see his expression even from across the facility, his desperate gasp before he dipped back under. A scream echoed briefly, seeming to come from nowhere. Dean emerged again about a foot away, clutching his son to his chest. It was clear that Dean wasn't a strong swimmer as he paddled with one arm toward the pool's edge and hung there on the tiled lip while the waves rocked him. Ian's wails rang out intermittently in the din.

Claire, the lifeguard on wave pool duty, was now crouched at the edge of the pool, pointing an accusatory finger and shouting at the teenagers. One of them, a girl with a stringy wet ponytail sticking out the top of her head, raised her hands in a "What gives?" gesture and then turned away, shaking her head. She conferred with the others, and the five of them then swam toward the shallow end and sauntered their way out of the pool.

Dean followed suit and began to awkwardly splash toward the shallow end, his son's face buried in his neck. Claire threw him a buoy, and he slapped the water a few times to secure himself on it, finally paddling to a place where he could safely walk. As the water streamed off his body, he seemed to shrink under its weight. He was coming toward Gavin now, and Gavin could clearly see the look on Dean's face as he stole glances at the teenagers on the deck walking toward the hot tub, laughing and deliberately ignoring his stares. But Dean's expression was not one of anger, as Gavin had expected. His lip quivered like a child's, his body loose and deflated, spent from the ordeal. Meanwhile, his son clung to him with abandon, pressing every part of himself to his father's skin.

Gavin watched them slip into the men's change room. He followed. He didn't know why; he felt responsible, though he knew it had had nothing to do with him. He wanted to make it better somehow.

But when he turned the corner into the locker area, he couldn't see Dean anywhere. A grey-bearded guy stood naked at his locker, his dimpled buttocks jiggling as he rummaged through his things.

Another guy was putting on his sneakers. Two boys whipped towels at each other. Gavin walked the aisles and scanned the changing stalls for closed doors. There, at the end of the hall, a pair of white feet was visible beneath one of the doors.

He approached and stood by the adjacent change room, waiting. What would he say? He would start by asking if Ian was okay, although the sounds coming from behind the door suggested he was not. The boy was still sobbing softly, and Dean was saying something. It was not words, but a noise. *Chicka chicka chicka shhhh.* Over and over again. *Chicka chicka chicka shhhh.* A train noise, perhaps? Under the door, the feet stood still. Just one pair, white and smooth, like the feet of a statue. Gavin wondered where the son was, then realized Dean must be holding him, rocking him. *Chicka chicka chicka shhhh.* Gavin listened and waited. It was soothing, like a lullaby. The boy's whimpers were slowly quieting. The sound continued, looping around itself, an unbroken rhythm echoing on the tiled walls. Gavin waited for what felt like ten or even fifteen minutes.

Without warning, the door swung open, and there was Dean's face, looking straight at him. *Chicka chicka chicka shhhh.* For a moment Dean appeared to be performing a brilliant act of ventriloquism; his lips stayed pressed firmly together while the noise continued. *Chicka chicka chicka shhhh.* But then Gavin saw the fan. There it was, mounted in the ceiling above the stall. The blades jerked and whirred.

"Oh, hi," Dean said. He had his coat draped over his arm, and his son was sitting on the fold-out changing table, kicking his rubber boots and smiling as though nothing had happened.

"Sorry," said Gavin. "Uh … I just wanted to say that I really liked your class."

"Oh, yeah?" Dean looked at him queerly. "Well, thanks. I enjoyed reading your paper."

♦

That summer, Butter Buns inexplicably disappeared. Gavin didn't even know exactly when it happened. He'd become accustomed to averting his eyes from the poster when he walked past the open door of the room so as not to accidentally catch Arnie's vacant gaze. But one day, he noticed in his peripheral vision that something seemed different. It didn't dawn on him until he examined the wall and saw the four tiny thumbtack holes, the only evidence left behind, that Arnie was gone.

"Thank god," he said aloud to himself. He would no longer have to cringe when he brought friends down to the basement to play video games, fearful of the possibility that one of them would see the poster, prompting shrieks and jokes about Gavin beating off to the Terminator. He should have felt relieved, but for some reason, he didn't. Instead, he felt a little bit sad.

His mother never did say anything about it, and Gavin never asked. He wanted to find out what had happened to the poster but couldn't think of a way to ask his mother without suggesting that he had in fact liked it and even missed it now. The room seemed entirely different without it, and he found himself trying to recall the poster's details: the gap-toothed grin on Arnie's face, the black Speedo pulled taut as a second skin, the way his clenched fists looked as though they should be holding something—an oar, a prize turkey, a bunch of balloons—that had been photoshopped out of the picture. The more Gavin thought about it, the campiness of the image was actually endearing. There was something honest about it that he had failed to see before.

Butter Buns's absence didn't seem to have any effect on his mother. She went down to the weight room every evening after dinner as usual, and once when Gavin stole a peek at her while she worked on her bicep curls, he saw that she stood facing the empty wall where Butter Buns had once watched over her. She was wearing a sports bra and Spandex pants, and even from a distance, Gavin could see the veins that had begun rising to the surface and rivering down her arms. By now, she'd gained enough muscle to turn heads when she walked down the street. Even her neck had become thick and sinuous, making her head appear stuck on top and pushed down too far, like a broken Barbie doll's.

Gavin imagined where the poster had gone—buried under porcelain cats at a thrift store, or pinned up in someone else's basement, or, most likely, dumped in a landfill at the edge of the city, tossed atop a heap of bloated plastic bags, plastic parts, discarded food rotted down to oozing black and green lumps. Arnie's body arcing backward over the pile, his grin pointed up at the useless sky.

Fixer

I KNEW I LIKED HER BETTER THAN SHE LIKED ME because that was often the way it was for me with popular women. Mariko was quick witted and intelligent, up on all the social media trends, and adept at exuding a genuine interest in others—all the things I wished I was. I was too worried about being liked to be likeable, and to be around me was to be less cool by association. So, I spent those six weeks seeking her out at the library and sitting where she always sat, in front of the windows that offered a panoramic view of the mountains. I stole chances to chat with her between work sessions, during which she wrote diligently, fingers gliding across her laptop keyboard, while I pretended to be researching contemporary portraiture instead of scrolling Facebook every five minutes.

We were both there on self-directed residencies—hers for poetry, mine for photography—among artists of various disciplines, all freed during our time there from the demands and expectations of real life. Our buffet meals were cooked for us by professional chefs, our beds were made each morning, and we were given unfettered

24-7 access to studios with state-of-the-art equipment. The luxury of it all was enough to make me feel a bit queasy at first, but like everyone else, I settled into a kind of charmed existence. It was like we'd all become young again, so it shouldn't have surprised me that a social order quickly developed. The twentysomethings were the fresh up-and-comers, the ones with the real ideas, while those with families and steady work back home were admired, but stale. I fell somewhere in between.

My last exhibition had been a photomontage series featuring competitive swimmers midrace. I'd taken the photos with a long shutter speed so that the images were blurry, all turquoise pool water and lithe ghostlike bodies swooping and torpedoing. It was, truth be told, basically a David Hockney rip-off and unsurprisingly got a lukewarm reception in my hometown. To summarize, I overheard a student of one of my former professors say to her friend as she stood in front of the title piece, "I mean, it's *pretty* and all ... but it feels kinda ... I dunno, blank, somehow. Like it's trying too hard."

Mariko, on the other hand, came from LA, and she wore a green velvet vest with an unaffected ease. She worked as a freelance writer and had sold articles to *The Atlantic* and GQ. A review of her first poetry collection called her writing "urgent" and "visceral." She had a kind of gravitational pull, so that within days of starting the residency, she already knew everyone—other writers, painters, even the digital media artists who holed themselves up in their studios all day. And she was young, only twenty-four, with a cool black undercut.

We met at the orientation dinner. I had an edge then because I knew one of the other artists, Katherine, from grad school, so we were sipping from our plastic wineglasses, reminiscing like old friends, even though we'd barely known each other back then. Mariko took the seat next to Katherine and shyly introduced herself. We told her we were photographers.

"Do you know Robert Mapplethorpe?" she asked, then quickly corrected herself. "What am I saying, of course you know Mapplethorpe." Her smile was a perfect crescent.

"Yeah, he's great," I said, immediately regretting such a pedestrian response.

"I was gonna say he has one of Patti Smith that I practically *worshipped*. I had it up on my wall since the fifth grade. It was completely ragged, but I just had to bring it with me to college."

I thought about how I'd liked Debbie Gibson in grade five, then realized Mariko was still talking but I was only half listening, mostly thinking about whether or not I could pull off an undercut. She had a small black star tattooed on her neck behind her left ear, which I couldn't stop looking at.

Katherine prattled about the project she was working on until Mariko interrupted, raising her hand like she was taking a vow.

"Embarrassing admission," she said. "I have no idea what that means."

"Oh, silver-based?" Katherine said. "Silver-based photography is black and white."

"Ah, I see. I didn't know there was silver involved. I mean, I have absolutely no idea how you make a photograph. None. Total child of the digital age."

"I'm still a believer in the superiority of film," I said.

"And making prints by hand is so much more rewarding," Katherine chimed in.

"Tell me all about it," Mariko said, leaning in. "Take me through the process. Silver-based photography. Step by step."

I let Katherine run through the darkroom basics: exposing a print by projecting light through a negative, and then putting the print through a series of chemical baths. She counted them off on her fingers: Developer. Stop bath. Fixer.

"The image emerges within seconds of immersion in the developer," she explained. "It kind of fades in slowly, like a Polaroid."

"Okay, yeah, I know what you mean." Mariko nodded.

"That's the most rewarding part," Katherine said. "Getting to see how it's turned out. Whether you got the exposure right, if there's enough contrast."

"Fascinating," said Mariko, the sparkle in her eyes suggesting that she really did mean it. I was emboldened.

"Nah," I cut in. "For me the most rewarding part is the fixer. The stop bath does exactly what it says: it stops the developer from acting on the print. Then comes fixer. The fixer strips off the unexposed silver and makes the image insensitive to any more light. That is where the photo really solidifies. Up until then it's so tentative, this ... image in limbo."

"I'm going to get another drink," Katherine said, standing up. "You need anything?"

"I'm good, thanks," I said.

"Me too," Mariko said, raising her half-full gin and tonic. I was relieved to watch Katherine wander away.

"So, what did you mean by that? Image in limbo?"

"Well, there's a kind of sharpening that happens in the fixer. It's not as dramatic a change as the developer, but you don't really know what the image looks like for sure until you fix it. And the fixing locks it in. No more uncertainty."

"Hm," Mariko said, looking off across the room. "I like uncertainty."

"Oh really?" I said.

"Yeah. Like in writing, if I knew where I was going all the time, I think all the energy would be taken out of it, you know?"

"True," I said, not knowing what else to say. I'd sounded like an ass just then, I realized. Like I had some kind of philosophy about my work, which I didn't. There were a few moments of silence. Mariko sipped her drink, then I did.

"I'm gonna go mingle some more," she said. "Wanna come?"

"Sure," I said, though I really didn't.

As the night continued, me standing sheepishly behind her, listening in on her conversations with other writers to which I had nothing to contribute, I realized I hadn't asked her anything about her work. At some point I found myself standing alone, drinking wine much too quickly and willing myself to look aloof yet not standoffish. This involved letting my free arm hang—not crossing it over my body—with just the right amount of slack to make the pose appear uncultivated. But after a few moments, I couldn't take it anymore, and no one was even making eye contact, so I retreated to my room before they brought out the tray of fancy mini desserts. I would hear about them later from Katherine, whom I spied having lunch with Mariko the very next day, the two of them giggling maniacally at something on Mariko's phone.

◆

I decided to bury myself in my work like all great artists are supposed to do, but it wasn't going well. I'd envisioned that returning to gelatin silver would herald a new kind of rawness in my work, a fresh start. I ended up focusing most of my efforts on half-heartedly browsing the work of other photographers instead of actually putting in time in the darkroom. My new project was a self-portrait series, and when I'd first conceived of it, I thought it would be so edgy and vulnerable because I was topless in the photos. But I was still hung up on the slow shutter speeds, and all the prints were coming across like a boudoir photo shoot gone wrong. And I couldn't even get the technicalities right. I was particularly unhappy about the nipples; each one seemed to pop out like a leering eyeball, no matter what I did. I wasted dozens of sheets of paper playing around with burning and dodging, burning and dodging. By the time each print made it into the fixer, the image just fell apart. Overexposed here, washed out over there. I thought about montaging them to cover up the shitty areas and salvage the decent stuff. Then I reminded myself I wasn't allowed to montage anymore. Meanwhile, Katherine worked alongside me, wearing her earbuds and humming to indie music I didn't recognize. Of course, she kept stealing peeks at my awful prints on the drying rack and periodically plucking out an earbud to deliver insincere compliments like "gorgeous" and "ooh, interesting." On principle, I took pains not to look at hers.

◆

After a couple of weeks, the hookups began. Of course, everyone knew who was sleeping with whom. Katherine was having nightly rendezvous with a printmaker named James, which was quite the scandal since he was married. Marjorie, a retired painter who lived in a geodesic dome in the Kootenays, was cozying up to Hilda, another retired painter whom everyone confused with Marjorie. Mariko began dating a ceramicist, Roland Clay. I refused to believe that was his real name, so I had a bad impression of him from the beginning. But thanks to the legacy of that cheesy pottery wheel scene with Patrick Swayze in *Ghost*, the ceramicists were considered the sexiest of us all. Roland wore the same torn red-flannel shirt every day and smoked clove cigarettes by the dozens, watching his own curl of smoke drift into the sky as he stood by the huge outdoor wood kiln, overseeing his creations. He made things that he called "vessels of Mesopotamian influence." When we took a tour of each other's studios, I checked out his work. He had everything laid out on a glaze-splattered table.

"I love this cup," I said, picking up one of his pieces by its delicate little ring-shaped handle.

"It's a bowl," he told me, taking it from my hands and setting it back down in its place.

"Oh," I said. "This bowl is lovely," I said, cradling another piece.

"That's a cup."

"Wow," I said. He didn't seem upset; he just tossed his long hair and busied himself with rearranging his display.

"Well, thanks," I said, as I crept out of his studio. He held up peace fingers.

Shortly after Mariko and Roland began dating, a group of us decided to go out for dinner at one of the restaurants in town, which was a twenty-minute drive away. Only two people in the group had brought their cars to the residency, so we carpooled. Somehow,

I ended up in Roland's car, a square-snouted '80s Chevy, while Mariko went in the white Prius with the four other women. Having spent four weeks confined to the residency campus, we were all a bit giddy about going on an outing in the real world. Everyone in Mariko's car had dressed up, wearing makeup and dangly earrings and bangles and clothes made of fine materials of no practical use in the studio. Mariko wore a silky black jumpsuit and red heels, and she'd styled her hair in an effortless swoop across her forehead. I hadn't thought to bring anything fancy, so I was just wearing tights and a long flowy tunic that could pass as a dress. Which was probably why I'd been elected to go with Roland—his car's interior was thick with dust, and the threadbare upholstery was infused with a smell like McDonald's cheeseburgers.

Our two cars caravanned down the highway into town, the Prius in front and us in back. I could see the women in the other car talking and laughing. Roland and I were mostly quiet. "Jasmine, dude!" Roland yelled as he tailgated the Prius. He knew she couldn't hear him, of course, so I guessed it was for my benefit. "It's a highway." He waved an arm. "The hell are they doing in there. What's the speed limit here, anyway? Gotta be at least ninety."

"I think a hundred," I said. "They seem distracted."

"Jessie's Girl" came on the radio, and Roland cranked it. He veered the car into the opposing lane and slammed on the gas. The Chevy choked and roared.

All four women turned their heads in unison as we sped up alongside them. Mariko gave Roland the finger.

"Oh, yeah?" Roland said, and suddenly he was pulling my head down into his lap, laughing. His jeans smelled like gravel, and I accidentally rubbed my teeth against them when I came down, so I discovered they tasted like gravel too. His hand held my head there, pressing my ponytail into my skull. My first impulse was to resist, but when I cranked my head around I caught him giving the other car a gangster-style nod, and then I understood what the joke was. I knew without looking that the women in the other car were laughing too. It was funny because I was so square, you see. To protest would only have proven them right. So I laughed too, the smell of the jeans and old cheeseburgers closing in around me.

It seemed to take forever for our car to pass the Prius and slide back into the lane. Rick Springfield's tinny voice blared from the speaker directly in front of my ear. I started to think we must be playing chicken with the opposing traffic, but when Roland released me and I sat up, the road was empty except for us. Towering pine trees rushed past on either side. Roland didn't say anything, just kept on grinning and looking back at the Prius behind. I was grateful he didn't look at me, because I was sure my cheeks were flushed.

"Who knew Jas drives like such a granny," he eventually said.

In town, when we got out of our cars, Roland threw his arm around Mariko and said, "You don't mind, baby?"

Mariko shrugged. "Why would I mind?" she said. "I'd tap that ass." And she pushed Roland away playfully and tucked an arm under mine, circling my waist. I did my best to behave as if I were a person to whom people were provocative all the time. We walked like that all the way from the car to the restaurant down the block.

◆

By week five, I'd decided to scrap my negatives and start again. I did another shoot, this time junking the slow shutter speed idea. *Just keep it simple*, I told myself. *Sharp lines. Make it about the image, just be real.* I used a timer to take the shots, which I thought would contribute to the spontaneity.

I happened to catch Mariko alone at lunch that day after finishing the shoot, and I was in a good mood over the potential of my new roll of film. I told her I was going to head to the lab right after lunch to develop the film.

"Oh my god, can I come?" she said. "I'm so thrilled for you. I'd just love to observe, you know, learn how it all works."

"Absolutely," I said. "It would be fun to show you." I assured myself that even if the film was bad, she wouldn't be able to tell; the negatives were too small for her to discern much.

I brought her to the developing lab and showed her the light outside that warned not to enter because development was in process.

"It's so intimate," she said. "Just us and the film, in the dark."

We got inside, and I set up my supplies while she sat on a stool and watched.

"So, obviously it's going to be dark," I explained. "You won't be able to see anything. But you'll hear the sound of my reel." I demonstrated. "I'll reel the film onto this so that I can put it in the canister, and once the funnel is in and screwed on, it's lightproof."

"But didn't you say there's a safelight?" she said. "Like a red lamp or something?"

"We can use a safelight when making prints, but film is much more sensitive. It's gotta be pitch black."

"So, you can do all of that in the dark?" she asked.

"I've had a lot of practice," I said. "Ready?"

"Yup," she said, standing up.

I flicked off the lights and found my way back to the counter where I'd set out my supplies. I began prying open the film cap.

"What's happening?" Mariko said, and I realized that she was standing right behind me.

"Just getting the film out now," I explained. I unfurled the ribbon of film and felt in the dark for her hand. "Here it is," I said as I tried to give it to her. But my hand was touching something else, something more solid. "Oh," I said, "sorry." I felt around until I got my bearings. A leg. A torso. She was rigid, standing like a tree. I realized I had touched her crotch. My hand had jabbed it, right on the bone. The thought of it sent a current up through me, like I'd just opened a soda can inside my body.

I touched her there again.

I didn't know what I was doing. I didn't think I was sexually attracted to her. I was just trying something.

Mariko kept still. I didn't know how to read her. It was dark, of course, and silent. So I stopped.

"Jesus," I said, "I can't seem to find your hand. There. You feel it?" I guided her hand to hold the roll by its end. "Just don't touch the negatives," I said. "Fingerprints."

She passed it back to me. "Neat," she said quietly.

When we emerged into the light, Mariko rubbed her eyes with her fists and blinked. There was a blob of yellow on her white shirt—a mustard stain—that glowed fluorescent as my eyes adjusted.

"Thanks," she said, already turning down the hall. "I promised Roland we'd get ice cream." She didn't look back.

◆

The new film didn't solve anything. In fact, it was worse than the original, or maybe it was partly the shame I felt every time I tested a print. My face in the photos, so self-satisfied, so sure of how sophisticated I would look. I wanted to burn them, one after the other. Take them out to the huge kiln behind the ceramicists' studio, lay each one on a metal tray and slide it through the oven door like a corpse.

On the last day of the residency, I saw Mariko again. She was in the library, in her usual place at the windows, reading a cloth-bound book and rocking back on her chair. Her bare toes were pressed up against the glass, and she kept pushing off of it, letting herself balance on the two back legs of her chair for a moment, then catching herself again with the tips of her toes. The sound was like a tiny bird trying to get in.

Wolf-Boy Saturday

"AL-MA," SHE SAID. "ALL-MA. CAN YOU SAY IT? ALLLL-MA."

That had been their first meeting. No other words. Just Alma and the boy in a small white room, looking everywhere but at each other. His mouth had hung open. His eye teeth, longer and pointier than normal, or perhaps she had imagined that.

"Alma Samar," said her resumé. Then, farther down, "people person." Both were lies. Samar sounded better than Grudensky, she'd thought, and she and Safi were practically married anyway. "People person" was something that all people put on their resumés. Alma had majored in linguistics, and somehow the volunteer coordinator at Sunshine Group Homes decided that this qualified her to teach someone—a boy, in fact, a mute boy—to speak.

"He's not disabled—I mean, he's *capable* of talking," Deborah, *call-me-Debbie*, had explained. "And he's been seeing all kinds of doctors," she went on, her eyes combing the crinkle in Alma's forehead. "Psychiatrists, psychologists, speech pathologists, you name it. He just needs a little warmth."

Alma had walked out of Sunshine Group Homes that morning chewing her lip, her teeth nibbling at hanging bits of skin like fish scales. Instead of going to her car, she walked past the parking lot, through Chinatown, and into Dragon City Market, drifting through narrow grocery aisles packed with the smells of ginseng and shiitake mushrooms. She walked through the cultural centre's golden pillars and over the bridge to Prince's Island Park. Then, sitting on a bench along the Bow River, where as a toddler she had torn crusts into tiny pieces and tossed them to the ducks, she read the file and felt sorry. Nobody fed the ducks anymore, not since they'd started shitting all over the manicured lawns, chasing little old ladies, squawking like deranged drug addicts. The world had finally figured out that it was wrong to feed wild animals; it made them nasty, dependent, like tantrumming children with no other tactics for getting their way.

Alma decided she'd give the boy some time. Saturday Jones—who'd given him a name like that?

Safi would be proud of her.

◆

Safi had taken the job up north seven months ago.

"You're going to go to hell," Alma had warned him. "Fort Mac is practically the devil's doorstep."

"I'm sorry," Safi had said, "but one of us needs a job." And so he put away his archaeology degree and became her provider, her big shiny driller, sending home the bacon every two weeks while Alma baked cookies, wrapped them in parchment paper, and FedExed them to the oil sands, where they would be shared like rations among grubby, callused fingers.

"You're sure you don't want to move out here with me?" The question came every Sunday as if on a timer, as if another six days might have been enough time for her to get lonely, desperate.

"I told you. There's nothing for me to do out there. Unless you want me to sit at home and knit mittens." The suggestion had sounded ridiculous the first time, but after ten months of job searching and three failed interviews, she was running out of sarcasm.

"Do some volunteer work, then," Safi said. The soft crackle of wax paper. Another hamburger, or maybe a Taco Bell burrito. "You should get out, meet some people. You can't stay holed up inside all the time."

Oh, but I can, she thought.

"I'm just not the volunteer type," she said instead. "All cheery and bubbly and, you know—"

"Selfless? Compassionate?"

"Please. Because *your* job is really helping mankind, right?"

No answer. The silences, the spaces of dead air between their lines, were growing longer, more frequent.

"You could work at a café," he finally said.

◆

She brought cookies to her second meeting with Saturday. Debbie met her at reception, looked at the Tupperware streaked with melting chocolate chips, and said, "Ohh." She touched Alma's forearm with one hand, took hold of the Tupperware with the other. Her fingernails were too long, the tips slightly yellow.

"That's sweet of you. But I'm going to have to ask you not to. Not yet. He's on a strict nutrition plan. Low sugar, high carbs. He was very malnourished."

"Of course, sure. No problem." She surrendered the cookies and watched Debbie pass them to the receptionist, who quickly tucked them away into a drawer.

"Besides," Debbie said, cocking her head like a budgie, "you want to *earn* his trust, don't you?" A big wide smile, sickly sweet as a piece of cake with too much icing.

Alma entered the white room and found Saturday sitting under the table. The door clicked shut behind her, and she stood against the blank wall, thinking, contemplating her first move. She thought back to people she knew with kids, to TV and movies with cheeky kid characters. In situations like this, adults were meant to be playful, beguiling.

"Oh my goodness," she said, setting her bag on the floor. "Where has he gone? Where on earth could Saturday be?" She swung her arm way out cartoonishly, brought her hand to her forehead like a visor, peered across the room as though she could see for miles. "He must've disappeared," she went on, her voice sounding warped, overinflated. She ambled around the room, looking from one corner to another.

"Hmm … hmmmm …" she said to herself as she mock searched, scanning the blank walls. Four whole minutes of this, and Saturday still didn't bite. He sat motionless under the table. Alma could see his ankles, his knees pulled up to chest, one arm wrapped under his thighs. She began to feel pathetic, like she was putting on a show, a bad sketch comedy. She forced a chuckle.

"Okay then, enough of that game." She got down on her knees and crawled toward him. He was clutching the table leg, his nose mashed into one of his fists. His dark eyes stared. His clothes—a T-shirt and green corduroys—were baggy and gathered in awkward lumps at the folds of his body. The clothes seemed more decorative than practical on him, like a dog in a tuxedo.

"Remember me?" Alma reached out to touch Saturday's shoulder, then thought better of it and let her hand drop to the floor. His eyes darted downward, watched her pointer finger scratch at the tile by his foot. He had something—something small and whitish grey—wedged in his fist. "What have you got there?" Alma asked. Can I see?" Saturday pressed his nose into it further, nuzzling. Alma could see a kind of fuzz, or perhaps fur, poking out between his fingers. *Christ*, she thought, *he's caught something. A mouse.*

"Now, Saturday," she said, "I need to see what you have there. Let me see." *Can you get rabies from mice?* she wondered. She reached out slowly, gently taking hold of his fist. He made a tiny noise. A squeak. It startled her, making her jerk her hand away.

"Shhh," she found herself saying, more to herself than to Saturday. "It's okay," she said. Just open your hand, like this. She held her fists in front of her and slowly opened her fingers, spreading them wide. "See?"

Saturday stared at her hands, frozen.

"See?" Alma said again, repeating the action over and over. No response.

Alma suddenly saw herself, the absurdity. Here she was, kneeling on a bare floor in an empty cell, expected to bond with this damaged child. Her roster of stereotypical bonding activities—flying a kite, getting ice cream cones, having a picnic, building a model airplane—had been nixed by Debbie. There would be security issues, Debbie had insisted. Risk of injury, overstimulation. Saturday needed stability and consistency. "Let's take it slow," she had said. "Talk to him, get him used to you, your voice." Alma had not realized that what Debbie really wanted was a fixture, a flesh-and-blood body that could park itself in the same room once a week and broadcast language, communicate by osmosis.

"For fuck's sake," Alma said under her breath. The words seemed to reverberate around her. She held her breath for a moment, listening to the stillness. It seemed that Saturday was holding his breath too, or if he was breathing, Alma could not hear it.

"Fuck," she said, louder.

Saturday blinked.

Without thinking, Alma snatched his hand and pried it open. A small shred of dirty cotton batting fell out of it. She caught only a quick glance before Saturday gathered it up again and balled it in his hand. He scurried to the opposite corner of the room and sat tucked against the wall, whimpering softly.

Alma stood up slowly, sat down in one of the hard metal chairs, and pulled herself up to the table as if she were about to have a meal. There were still forty-five minutes left in their session. Debbie would expect her to stay there, present, serene, like a sculpture. The important thing, Debbie said, was for Alma to signal her receptiveness. She could not leave; she was trapped.

◆

"He has something—a piece of fuzz," Alma told Debbie after the session. She wasn't sure what else to say. Debbie had wanted to meet in her office for a "debriefing," but she was madly filling out forms for grant applications that were due that afternoon. Her eyes were wide, glued to her computer screen.

"Hmm? Oh ... yes. That's his bankie," she said. The sound of her clawlike fingernails clicking the computer keys was like a spoon cracking an egg.

"His what?"

Debbie looked at Alma, sighed. "I'm sorry, I forget that not everyone has a lot of experience with small children. My kids all had bankies—that's what they call them. Security blankets, you know? They carry them everywhere."

"So ... it's a blanket?"

Debbie nodded.

"Where's the rest of it?"

"Ha ha, I guess you're right. I'm not explaining myself very well. It's just ... it sounds worse than it is."

"I'm not sure what you mean."

"It's from the previous volunteer, Glenda. She gave him a toy. A little stuffed lamb. It was very cute. Anyway, Saturday isn't accustomed to toys, as you might imagine. So he responded ... I guess in a way that Glenda didn't expect."

"What did he do?"

"He just tore it up a little." Debbie's words were pouring out more and more quickly, as though she were suddenly on fast-forward. "Pulled at the seams and tore the stuffing out. We had to throw it away. But for some reason, he kept a little piece of the stuffing. He seems to like the smell of it. So, I call it his bankie. I think it makes him feel safe."

"Oh. Okay."

"No need to worry yourself about it," she said, sifting through stacks of paper.

Right, Alma said to herself as she walked out the door. *A five-year-old viciously tore apart his toy and ripped out its insides. No big deal.*

◆

The last time she had visited Safi in Fort McMurray, they'd decided to "do as the locals do"—Alma's joke—and hang out at Tim Hortons. Safi had gained weight; his jeans were tight, the fabric pinching around the button. He ordered an "iced cap."

"You mean an iced cap*puccino*?" Alma corrected him at the till. She had on a crooked smile, one arched eyebrow. Safi just looked at her. The woman at the till cast her eyes down, pushed a button on her computer screen.

"Three seventy-seven. Anything else?" she said, not looking at either of them.

"You know, technically," Alma said to Safi as they made their way to a table, "a cappuccino is made of espresso, half milk, and half foam."

"Okay," he replied. "So?"

"So that slushy shit they're giving you? That's not a cappuccino. It's a coffee Slurpee."

"Well," he said, "I guess that's marketing for you."

Alma poked him in the shoulder. "I was only kidding," she said. "Teasing you." Except she knew she wasn't. Really, she was making a point. The Safi she knew would never utter the words "iced cap."

The former Safi would never have voluntarily sat in a Tim Hortons. He would never, ever, have hung out in a crowded fast food joint and fanned the Lifestyle section of the *Edmonton Journal* in front of him. But this Safi seemed entirely at ease doing those things. He sipped from his straw, tucked into the side of his mouth. He read as if he'd been playing out this sad routine for a lifetime.

"How's that kid?" he asked Alma.

"Crazy," she said. "Apparently they call them 'feral children.'"

"Alma," he said darkly.

"What?"

"That's not exactly PC, you know."

"What? That's what they call them. I did the research."

"You make it sound like he was raised by wolves or something."

"Look, I've got the dictionary open right now," she said, fiddling with her phone. "'Feral: in a wild state, especially after escape from captivity or domestication.'"

"Jesus, Alma, he was abused. He's not wild. Just scarred."

"Four years, Safi! He wasn't ever allowed to leave that little room. No friends. He wasn't even potty trained when they found him."

"All you have to do is talk, right? Who knows, maybe that helps. He's got psychiatrists for all the other stuff. You're like his buddy."

"More like his cellmate."

"That's ironic," Safi said.

"What do you mean? How?"

"Never mind, nothing. All I'm saying is that they must see something in you. They wouldn't have paired you up with him if they didn't think you could help him. Just try, okay?"

"You're such a saint," Alma said. "Makes me want to puke."

◆

"I got a job," she blurted as soon as Safi said hello.

"Wow, Al. That's great. In Calgary?"

"Of course," she said, annoyed that that was his first question. "Where else?"

"So what is it?"

"It's just a café job," she said. "You know, serving coffee, cleaning tables, sweeping up muffin crumbs. Not a real job or anything. But it's something, right?"

"Oh," Safi said. "I didn't know you were applying for jobs like that. In Calgary."

"Well, I took your advice, I guess."

"I guess," he said.

Alma said nothing.

"What about the kid?" Safi finally asked. "Your volunteering."

"I can still do it," Alma said. "I'm on shift work." Their phone conversations had begun to resemble calls to customer service, like troubleshooting with tech support. *Try this. No? Okay, how about this? Have you tried this?* You were stuck on the line, waiting for the answer, the magic fix, so you could finally hang up.

"So, it's going well then? Has he started to talk?"

"It's going great," she said. "Really good." She nodded to herself, hoping it would make her voice sound more convincing. "What are you eating?"

"Chubby Chicken," Safi said. "Sorry, it's greasy." Lips sucking fingers, one after another, a slippery melody.

Alma had skipped out on her meeting with Saturday to go to the job interview. *He won't miss me,* she'd told herself.

✦

She'd taken to showing up armed with books. Cardboard baby books, picture books, storybooks, even novels—anything she could use to fill up the time. Saturday wouldn't even look at them. He'd stare down at the floor or his lap, nuzzling and sniffing the stuffing in his fist.

"Treeee," she'd say, belabouring every page, tracing all the pictures. "Snow. See, snooow. See it falling from the sky?" Saturday's unresponsiveness was almost enough to make Alma believe that the words meant nothing at all.

Once, she read aloud twelve pages from *Pride and Prejudice.* When her voice got tired, she just sat across from Saturday, reading silently. After a while, she caught his eyes starting to follow her turning of the pages. *Breakthrough,* she thought to herself. *Debbie would probably be ecstatic.* She left that day without saying a word to her.

Later, when Alma stepped into the shower to get ready for her evening shift at the Heartland Café, she thought about Saturday's bankie. She too had once had a security blanket—a crocheted one, made by her mother. She'd worn it so thin that the yarn became loose and unravelled, and half of it eventually fell away. As a toddler, lying in her bed trying to fall asleep at night, she'd used to wrap the salvaged half around her hand, then coil it like a cobra around and around her wrist and all the way up her forearm. She had forgotten about this habit until now. She could not for the life of her remember what that comfort felt like, nor could she remember what had happened to the bankie. It seemed that one day it had been there, and the next it was gone. But she thought she recalled a flash memory of moonlight on her bare arm, a feeling of absence.

How odd, she considered, that Saturday had kept the shred of the toy he himself had destroyed. He'd rejected the toy, and yet he cherished its remains. The logic was faulty. He didn't want it, but still loved it. A piece of it. Perhaps, she reasoned, he'd thrown most of it away just so he could have something to miss.

When Alma got out of the shower, Safi was sitting on the couch.

"Surprise," he said. He gestured toward a vase full of gaudy red roses, complete with a baby's breath accent, on the coffee table in front of him. He knew nothing about flowers.

"Jesus," Alma said, clutching the towel to her body. "You scared the crap out of me."

"Sorry," Safi said. "But wasn't it romantic?"

Alma leaned down and kissed him, her wet hair falling out of the wrapped towel and swatting his face.

"Sure," she said, smearing the water off his cheek. She suddenly felt cranky; she didn't have the time to entertain him. "It was very nice of you to come. But I have to work tonight. I have to go in about fifteen minutes."

"Can I come?" he said.

"Can you come? Come to the café and watch me serve people? No."

"Why not? I'll read."

"I never asked to come to your work," she said. She pictured herself in a yellow hard hat and boots thick with mud, peering into a never-ending hole. It was then that she realized she had no inkling what Safi actually did all day. "Besides, it's embarrassing."

"Oh, come on. I know you're actually a brilliant linguist. Tell me all that stuff again about the signifier and the signified. I can't remember which is which."

"Yeah, yeah, later. Although I'm sure you're dying to hear it."

"Look," Safi said, stopping her as she tried to leave the room, "I want to come. Really. I'm worried about you."

"Worried?" Alma rolled her eyes. "Why?"

"You sent back my letter? With the cheque?"

"I didn't need it," she said. "I'm working now."

"Yes, but … for minimum wage, Al."

"I get tips."

"Alma. You need the money."

She felt hot and cramped, like her muscles were being reeled up under her skin.

"The signifier," she said, "is the word *money*. The signified is what the money means."

Safi stared at her, his mouth slightly open. She hated his face in that moment. He was trying to make her feel unreasonable, ridiculous. "Is that supposed to be funny?" he said.

"Am I laughing? I need to get ready. My hair is still wet. I don't know why you're here."

"Me neither," he said, standing.

"You know I hate cut flowers," Alma said. "I've told you that. Several times."

"You're being a bitch," Safi said.

"You're spitting," she replied. "You just spat on my arm."

"I'm going to my parents'," he said, tossing the cheque on the table. "Call me when you can control yourself."

✦

Debbie gave Alma a sandwich to feed to Saturday. Ham and cheese on white bread.

"See if he takes it," she said, as though it were some kind of elixir.

Saturday was sitting at the table when Alma came in. He watched her come toward him with her hands behind her back. He knew what was coming. A treat.

"Here you go," Alma said, unwrapping the plastic and laying the sandwich on it.

Saturday snatched the slice of bread off the top and began breaking it into little pieces, which he arranged around the table like puzzle pieces. He ate them one by one, slowly, deliberately. Then, he unpacked the rest of his sandwich, layer by layer—the bread, each slice of cheese, the single round slice of ham—and ate the bread and cheese the same way, breaking them into small chunks, popping one after another into his mouth. The ham, he left intact.

Alma didn't try to speak. Saturday's actions were mesmerizing—so calculated and careful that they seemed alien, mismatched to the frail, anxious child possessed by them.

When he picked up the ham, he looked at Alma briefly, his eyes searching, questioning. Then he brought it under the table. *Is he going to save it?* Alma wondered. *Put it in his pocket?* But he was looking down at his lap. His hands seemed busy.

Alma came around the side of the table and knelt beside Saturday. He was wearing a pair of faded camo-print shorts, and one pantleg was hiked up, exposing his bare thigh. Stuck to the skin was the slice of ham, pink and glistening. On first glance, Alma pictured the skin cut away, the muscles exposed. Saturday was smoothing the ham out against his thigh, grazing it with his finger as though it were a small animal, like a guinea pig. Then, he pulled up the edge, peeled it back a little, and let it flop back down, making a soft slapping sound, flesh against flesh. He petted it again, smoothing it out to the edges. Peel slap smooth, peel slap smooth, over and over.

The sound spread around the room, filling the space. It was rhythmic, but there was something dooming about it. When Alma closed her eyes, the sound became rough, like scraping. It was a soundtrack to the scene in her head: a vast hole in the grey earth, a trench, excavators parked precariously along its slopes with arms raised as though frozen in time. She saw herself standing at the edge, wondering how it would ever be finished.

Old Wives

LAST NIGHT, I FOUND AN EARWIG in the glass that holds our toothbrushes. Turned the glass upside down, toothbrushes spilling in the sink. I trapped the earwig and left it there. Watched it carousel around the glass before I went to bed.

It wasn't cruel, because earwigs can pinch. They can crawl into your orifices, lay eggs in your skull.

On our RV vacation last year, Dan and I visited the natural history museum in Boston. Dan's arthritis and my bad hip had been acting up, but Dan didn't want to miss the meteorites. We doddered through a maze of taxidermied animals—cougars and antelope and exotic birds and ancient Asian elephants, their old, dry skins splitting at the seams. In one room we saw beetles, hundreds of them, pinned to the wall in a hierarchical triangle.

Wouldja look at that? Dan had said, scratching his chin. *All the colours of the rainbow.*

I smiled, but they were not beautiful to me. What was the point, I wondered, in seeking out each and every species of beetle, naming it, finding its niche, then killing and displaying it, inert, behind a pane of glass? Dead but intact, like a crime scene. I didn't know what I was supposed to feel, looking at those beetles.

I remembered how when I was young, before I had a mother's heart, I'd caught dragonflies in jars and shook them to death. Sometimes I'd added a rock to the jar, and afterward, the broken wing pieces tinkled like chips of nail polish. Once, when I couldn't find a rock, I'd poured the dead dragonfly out on the sidewalk and tried to pull the wings off. The body split down the centre. Flesh pink as ham.

The next week, we were in Chicago, and at the natural history museum, there was the same display. The same pinboard of beetles shining like candies. We both stood for a moment, looking at it, then moved on without a word.

Something was lost for Dan, I knew. He's not stubborn like me, doesn't cling to fantasies. For him, the beetles in Boston had been magical ingredients, gathered together and categorized—parasites, scavengers, fungivores, carnivores, herbivores—and Dan had created a little world in his mind, a beetle village where every character had a name, a special role. To see the same beetles again, duplicated, somehow made them insignificant. As if they cancelled each other out.

This morning, the earwig was gone, the glass turned upright. A crumpled bit of toilet paper in the trash. Dan hadn't said anything. Back when our kids still lived at home, he might have said, *Well, Rhonda, were you going to tell me about your little pet in the bathroom?* He would have explained that earwigs are harmless, then taken the glass outside and flung the insect to the wind.

We've learned to say only what is necessary. Dan knew that if he'd set the earwig free, I would never have touched my lips to the glass again.

Siberpoo

EUGENIE COULDN'T STOP MULLING OVER THE WINEGLASS.
Though the dinner had been eaten and the plates cleared and the
conversation had long ago shifted to Maxine's miniature poodle and
his habitual late-night liaisons with a neighbouring cocker spaniel,
still Eugenie ruminated on the way Maxine had carelessly poured
the champagne with her glass raised way up, winking in the hot sun,
while Leonard was bent at her feet, mopping up the spill from the
bottle, which had only stopped frothing moments before. The crack
of the wineglass shattering on the porch had brought the chaos of
the scene to its pinnacle: Leonard doubling over, performing a gra-
tuitous somersault into the smoking barbecue, yelping like a hyena,
and Maxine hollering "Opa!" as she plucked shards of glass from
the puddle with blue-nailed fingers. Eugenie had bustled around
them like a little tornado, sweeping up the glass and Dustbusting
the stray shards and wiping Leonard's splattered pantleg and rolling the barbecue into the corner before returning, without a glass
for herself, to join the toast to Charlie's tenure appointment at the

university. The frantic energy Maxine and Leonard created when they were together was a kind of monstrous alchemy; even now, as they sat across the patio table from one another, Maxine umbrellaed by the wide brim of her black French hat and Leonard shielded behind sunset-orange mirrored sunglasses, an unrelenting intensity hung in the air between them, an eyeless stare that each was aiming at the other.

"Don't they call that a cockapoo?" Charlie offered, smiling his lopsided smile.

The wineglass had been a gift from Eugenie's sister. After hearing Charlie chaff about Eugenie's penchant for breaking wineglasses, Paula had insisted that the thinner and more delicate the crystal, the bowlier the goblet, the narrower the stem, the more careful attention Eugenie would pay to it, handling it with only the nimblest touch. Indeed, all six of the fragile wineglasses Paula had bought at great expense had remained intact, polished to spotlessness after each use and displayed on the open shelf where Charlie could see them—until today.

"But really," Maxine went on, "who are we to deny them their carnal pleasures? It's castration, after all. We don't use that term except in the context of torture."

"You think you're torturing him by keeping him tied up in the yard," Leonard said.

"Keeping him tied up in the yard!" Maxine said, not to Leonard but to Margot, and raising her hands in hyperbolic indignation. "Would you do that to a human and call it anything other than torture?" she said, and Margot laughed and shrugged in a polite, docile way.

Eugenie had suggested glass tumblers for the champagne, apologizing for the absence of flutes, and pointed out that champagne was best served in a narrow vessel so that the bubbles would have a longer path to travel up to the surface, making a more pleasing spectacle for the drinker. Maxine, however, had only laughed and accused her of being "too cute," then forked the delicate stems of two wineglasses between the fingers of each hand, necking them against one another. Eugenie made a sound of protest—*wope*—before turning away and letting Maxine sashay out the door and into the grey smoke puffing from the barbecue.

"Genie," Maxine said, snapping her fingers in Eugenie's direction. "You're with me, right?"

"I don't really know anything about dogs," Eugenie replied, swallowing her bitterness. She felt drained, exhausted from the heavy meal and the summer heat and the conversation that looped around itself like a tired old ribbon. All that now sustained her was the vague hope that the children would fade early after a long week of beach excursions, bike rides, and extravagantly heaped ice cream cones and come running from the playroom to compel the parents to dissolve some calamity over which girl got to wear which tiara or which tangled wig.

"I saw a new one the other day," Tony said. "A huskypoo. Is that a new one? I'd never seen one before."

"Yes, it's newer." Maxine nodded, choking a little on her drink in her haste to reply, and wiped bubbles from her upper lip. "Siberian husky poodle cross. High-energy breed, but hypoallergenic. They call it a Siberpoo also."

"Siberpoo?" Margot repeated. "Ha! That sounds so ... synthetic. Like something manufactured. I suppose it is, though."

"Siberpoos, definitely," Maxine said. "I mean, a little poodle and a huge husky? It's gotta be done by artificial insemination. Turkey baster, in other words."

"There's a fun job for you," Tony said, to which Maxine promptly retorted, "It's actually not all that difficult to get the bitch to comply. Let's face it, it's better than getting nothing."

Leonard had been quiet, and he leaned back in his chair and stretched out, his lips curled up in an impish smile. He knew what was coming, of course, as they all did: a proposal for the latest project, delivered by Maxine in a public venue, through which he would be caught, for how could he, without betraying a churlishness of which Maxine had accused him on several occasions, dismiss her?

"I've been doing a lot of research," it began, Maxine straightening up and laying her palms flat on the table. "As you know, I've had time on my hands."

Maxine had been let go from her position at the gallery and had spent the last nine months oscillating between states of feigned helplessness and manic ambition, always punctuated by some chimeric scheme to make money that fizzled into reverie as quickly as it had arisen. Leonard had called Eugenie a saint for the way she patiently handled Maxine during what he called her "blue periods," when she wept to Eugenie over the phone about rosemary shampoo that made her gag, the loud vacuuming of her landlady (with whom, to Maxine's ruination, they shared a wall), and her five-year-old daughter Penelope's insistence in singing and chattering incessantly while lying splayed out on the filthy floor with her colouring book and markers strewn around her. Eugenie had faithfully attended to Maxine's calls, sometimes in the middle of meetings or the middle of the night, absorbing the stories Maxine recounted as proof of Leonard's overbearing nature and relaying them back to her in altered form, revealing the concern and tenderness at the heart of his actions. She had brought Maxine a special blend of rare herbal tea to replace the prescription Ambien that Maxine insisted was a form of mind control, arranged for after-school care for Penelope at a nearby home daycare, and, without a hint of judgment, helped Maxine hang up some old saris in the corner of her bedroom to construct a meditation space where Maxine could "find ground."

"Anyone for some beer?" Charlie interjected, rising from the table and sandwiching the rims of two empty wineglasses between his fingers. Eugenie shot him a look of such roiling outrage that he quickly set them down again. It was clear to Eugenie, and to Tony and Margot, who nodded zealously at Charlie's offer and shifted in their patio chairs in tandem, anticipating their extended captivity, that Charlie was making a tactful escape, and Eugenie was doubly incensed by his heedlessness to her concerns about the glasses and his opportunism, which had been swifter than hers. Leaving the glasses, he slipped quietly into the house, and Leonard took his chance to split the conversation by telling Tony about the film he and Maxine had seen last weekend on their "date night"—a measure that Maxine had recently instituted at the behest of their marriage counsellor, whom Maxine claimed gazed at Leonard with a disturbing, lusty look every time he described his feelings in a session.

"The dialogue was just so *pedestrian*," Leonard complained, grimacing as though wounded. The expression encapsulated his approach to writing reviews as a drama critic; they almost always involved a vicious analysis of some aspect of the play, expressed as though it were a personal slight against him. Eugenie could see Tony's shoulders stiffen as he nodded and listened, no doubt because Tony and Eugenie had just had an earlier conversation with Maxine in which she gushed over the authenticity of the film and how the characters spoke like real people, without any of that pretentious Woody Allenesque cleverness of which everyone, especially Maxine, had grown so bored. Tony fiddled with one of the empty glasses that had been set down in front of him, sliding his fingers up and down the stem. He did so absently, listening, as was clear from the far-off look on his face, to both Leonard's scathing critique and Maxine's promulgation of her knowledge of breeding methods and breeding terminology—"quite easy to identify the heat cycle … and then a simple whelping box … but they call that 'outcrossing' …"—but not really listening. He was bracing himself, holding his jaw tight in an almost imperceptible cringe.

"There's virtually no cost up front," Maxine went on. "Even for a cheapskate, it's entirely reasonable."

"And the main character," Leonard continued, "the one played by Naomi Watts? Insufferable. I don't know if it was the writing or just the direction, but it was just so … tiresome! Overacted, desperate, exaggerated to the point of histrionic!"

"Poodle mixes are considered designer breeds right now. They're hot," Maxine said, snapping her fingers again. Charlie returned to the table with a decorous smile and four frosty glasses of beer, setting them down one by one at the centre of the table, encircling the hole where the umbrella stand would go if they had one. Looking at the hole made Eugenie realize that although they had invited their friends over to celebrate Charlie's success, he had by now been completely eclipsed. Her heart swelled with pity and love for him.

"Of course, the muttonheaded critics ate it up," Leonard said, pausing to gulp his beer. "Because, you know, this style is 'in vogue' right now." He used air quotes to signal his ironic use of *in vogue*, which he had also done earlier when telling Eugenie about Maxine's use of the word *sexy* to describe the old claw foot tub in their bathroom, remarking that what passed for fashionable these days was simply anything that had been passé twenty years ago. Leonard and Maxine had sold their house in the East Village to ease their financial burden and, for the last three months, had been living what Maxine romanticized as "the bohemian lifestyle," renting a suite off the side of an old heritage home downtown. It had only one large, open space that combined the kitchen, living room, and sleeping area, and there was no shower—a travesty to Leonard, who called bathing wasteful (citing seventy gallons of water for a single bath versus twenty-five gallons for a shower) and insisted that it added an extra twelve minutes to his morning routine, which he couldn't afford now that they'd moved fifteen minutes farther away from his office. Eugenie had invited Leonard to use the shower at her and Charlie's house, which he had done on several occasions. After the last time, Charlie had shaken his head and said to Eugenie, "You care too much about other people's problems."

Though it was now surely past seven—had they been sitting for an hour, maybe two?—the air around them was thick with heat and so dry that it gave Eugenie a chalky feeling inside her mouth, but for some reason she could not will herself to get up and fetch a glass of water, not even as the distant screams of children and Maxine's impassioned gesticulations and Leonard's persistent rocking back and forth on the rear legs of the chair, once even rocking himself so far backward so that he had to catch himself by grabbing the edge of the table, which sent the glasses wobbling and clinking together before mercifully shuddering back onto their bases, were fomenting in her a sensation of panic that made her heart beat in her eardrums.

"I'll go," Margot said, trotting inside the house to dispel whatever trivial quarrel had befallen the children in the playroom.

There was a moment of silence. They listened to the cries of the children rise in volume, then settle. And, in that small reprieve, everything became clear to Eugenie.

The glass had been broken on purpose.

Maxine and Leonard did not actually want her delicate diplomacy; they did not want Eugenie to stitch up the rifts between them. They wanted the rifts, revelled in the spectacle that tore through them. The dinner party had all been carefully orchestrated—every line, every response, every small gesture aimed at the other like a dagger working its way up the vertebrae, one by one.

"I think it's cruel," Eugenie announced. "Forcing two things together that don't belong together."

But then, Eugenie herself had also been part of it. She'd suggested inviting their friends over, to celebrate Charlie, yes, but also to suss out the state of things between Maxine and Leonard. They were like a sun—in a constant state of fusion and reaction, always on the precipice of some transformation that threatened to slowly absorb the planets surrounding it. You wanted to keep looking at it, even when it was blinding.

The three girls ran from the house then, grinning and springing into the laps of their respective fathers, with Margot following behind.

Leonard smoothed his daughter's hair and turned her on his knee to face him. "Now, Penelope. What do you think?" he said. "Would you want a Siberpoo?"

Penelope giggled and repeated the word with extra emphasis on the *poo*, sending the other two children into a fit of giggles as well, but when Leonard continued to look into her face, awaiting an answer, she scrunched up her nose and looked to her mother for a clue.

Maxine's face seemed to crumble like a dropped pie, and she pressed it into her palms as tears gushed forth. The table immediately went into a flurry, children scurrying, and their parents flying out of their chairs and trading positions round the table, Margot cupping Maxine's shoulder with one hand and kneeling down in front of her, Tony collecting the children in the net of his open arms, and Charlie taking Leonard aside, both men sliding their hands into their pockets.

"See, do you see?" Maxine sobbed, but Eugenie was no longer watching. She was already partway through the door, carving herself from the scene with the *schwick* of the latch, the frosty bite of the air conditioner catching in her throat and filling her with new air—a kind of dissolution she had never really believed in until now.

Porcelain Legs

A SINGLE HAIR.

It grew, long and wiry, out of the skin above Mom's almond eye, just above the crease of her eyelid. The kind of hair you'd expect to see on a toilet seat and not on someone's face. Did she know it was there? Queenie wondered. Didn't she care?

When the hair first appeared, it looked like a tiny check mark drawn with a mechanical pencil. You could have mistaken it for a stray eyebrow hair, plucked that morning, that had escaped the swipe of her hand. But then it grew longer, thicker, started to catch the light the way a beetle's back shines. Soon, the end of the hair hooked into a coil, twisting itself into a crimp along its length. Then, another crimp. It grew long enough to dangle, to rest against her eyelashes.

"Your dad was at the recital, did you see him?" Mom ladled black bean sauce over Queenie's rice.

"Yeah," Queenie said, taking the ladle from her hand. "I want more pork."

"How come you keep looking down at the table? It's rude. You look at people when they talk to you." Mom set her bowl down, picked up her chopsticks. The hair jogged along her eyelashes when she blinked. She absently whisked her palm across her face, the chopsticks sticking out of her fist. "Why were none of your friends there?"

"It's just Kiwanis, Mom. Lots of kids have recitals. No one cares."

"No one cares. You always say that. What kind of friends do you have?"

Queenie shrugged. "They have other things to do on weekends. Soccer and dance and stuff."

"Hm," Mom said, looking over her bowl, which she held under her chin. The end of the hair was now combed between two eyelashes, hovering in front of its reflection. It tugged gently on her eyelid each time she lowered her eyes back to her bowl. She chewed her rice thoughtfully, smacking her lips. "We talked to your teacher after."

"I know. I saw."

"She didn't believe that your dad was actually your dad." Mom snickered, revealing a ball of rice between her teeth.

"No one ever does."

"Anyway, she said your rhythms were excellent."

"That's good."

"Weren't you having trouble with the rhythms before?" She put down her bowl, swept her eye twice with her fingers.

"No."

"I thought you said the rhythms were hard."

"No, I said the time signatures were hard."

"Oh." She shrugged. "I thought it was the same."

Queenie rolled her eyes.

Mom sighed, picked something out of her teeth with a long pinky nail. The hair rested against the fan of her eyelashes. "It was nice of your dad to come. He said it was really good. He thought you were so good."

The hair was still there two days later—longer, crimpier. It spent most of its time brushed across Mom's eyelid, clinging to the skin. Every so often it wandered down, dangling, threatening to fish in the wet of her eyeball.

When Mom got home from work, she went straight into the kitchen, heels clicking against the tile, and started unpacking her lunch bag like she always did. Queenie was sitting at the kitchen table, eating Ritz crackers and cheese. Mom took out her Tupperware and placed it in the sink, paused to rub her eye. It was bloodshot.

"My eye is itchy," she said, pointing it at Queenie. "Does it look infected?"

Queenie picked up a cracker, nibbled the edge. "There's a hair there."

"What? What do you mean?" Mom walked right up to her, brought her face level with Queenie's.

"Right there." Queenie pinched the hair between thumb and finger. The feel of it reminded her of the dog hairs she always had to pick off her sweater after she walked the neighbour's German shepherd, Moby. The eyelid skin tugged.

"Ow." Mom jerked back. She fingered her eyelid, pinching at the skin. Finding the hair, she pressed it between her thumb and middle finger, gliding her fingertips down its length. "It's so long," Mom said, half smiling. She released the hair suddenly, pulled up a chair next to Queenie, and sat down. "Pull it out," she said, thrusting her face forward and closing her eyes.

"Pull it out?"

"Yes, just pull on it."

Queenie's fingers gripped the hair firmly. She pulled. The skin stretched.

"Ow, ow. Get it. Ow. Pull it."

"Ew. It's not coming out," Queenie said, releasing the hair. It stuck out straight.

Mom clucked her tongue, huffed. She hurried upstairs, leaving her heels pointed squarely at the bottom step.

Queenie and Erica had the cubbyhole that day. The cubbyhole was really just an alcove in the brick wall along the outside of the school. There was a red door at the end of it that was always closed. It was dark in there, and deep enough that a dozen kids could huddle inside it to escape the biting winter wind. But over the years, it had become tradition for the grade sixers to use it for escaping the eyes of teachers instead.

Way back in September, Erica had worked it out with Ryan, Jesse, and Aaron that the boys could have the cubbyhole on Mondays and Wednesdays, and she, Becky, and Queenie could have it on Tuesdays and Thursdays. The boys said no way at first, but Erica had made them all gather around her in the cubbyhole, making a wall with their bodies. *Make a wall, make a wall,* she had said, and they all asked her why, what was she doing, but she just giggled and kept motioning with her hands. Once the three boys, Becky, and Queenie had surrounded Erica, blocking the light so that only the dim glow pouring over their heads shone on her body, she grabbed the hem of her skirt and whisked it up, holding it in clenched fists under her chin.

They all gasped.

Erica stood motionless, her eyes gazing directly ahead, a tight smirk stretched across her face. Her panties were white and patterned with tiny red hearts, but the fabric was worn thin so that her skin showed through in patches, and some of the hearts had turned pinkish. Queenie could see the faint grey line down the middle of her crotch.

Ryan and Jesse clapped their hands over their mouths and burst into hysterical laughter. Slivers of light filtered through the gaps between their legs and danced about Erica's naked thighs, illuminating the tiny white hairs stippling her skin.

An image flashed in Queenie's mind: the porcelain doll her aunt had given her years ago. The doll had black hair and dark-brown eyes, just like Queenie's. She stood out on the shelf among Queenie's other six dolls, her flat brown eyes staring. *It's a Chinese doll,* her aunt had said when Queenie opened it. Yes, Queenie had noticed that the doll's eyes were slightly upturned at the corners. But when she lifted the doll's yellow taffeta skirt, there was a pair of white porcelain legs. So white, so smooth, so thin that Queenie had been afraid they'd shatter if she held them too hard.

Queenie looked at Becky. Becky wasn't smiling. She was staring, eyes vacant, at Erica's face, her lips parted slightly. Queenie thought Becky looked worried. Scared.

Erica opened her fists and allowed her skirt to drop. Her smirk cracked into a big smile as the boys ran away, still hysterical with laughter. With the boys now gone, daylight poured into the cubbyhole, glinting against Erica's glossy teeth.

Queenie and Becky stared at her, holding their elbows.

"What?" Erica said, brushing her palms together. "Now it's a deal."

The boys let them have Tuesdays and Thursdays after that, and Fridays were for whoever could get there first. The last two Fridays, Queenie had claimed the cubbyhole because she was the first one let out of class, having finished her assignments early. So now Erica and Becky called Queenie "the champion" and patted her on the back when the boys came, sneering. Erica and Becky had also let Queenie hang out with them for the whole of recess every day last week and this week.

Today was a cold December Thursday, and Becky was at home sick. Queenie and Erica leaned against the wall of the cubbyhole, taking their snacks out of their jacket pockets with mittened hands. Erica's legs were so long that she could plant her foot against the opposite wall and hold herself up. She liked to show Queenie and Becky, and she always made them try too, even though neither of them could ever do it. Without Becky there, Erica put one foot up against the wall, but she didn't ask Queenie to try.

"I'm doing this fashion show thingy at the mall," Erica said. "On Saturday. Wanna come?" She poured a little pile of Wheat Crunch in her mitten and tossed it into her mouth.

Queenie reddened, her eyes growing wide. "Well, I don't really know anything about modelling."

Erica giggled. "No, I mean just to watch. You have to be *recruited* to model." Her pillowy bottom lip puckered out when she said "recruited." "It gets kinda boring in the breaks between shows. They make us stick around, but we can go walking around the mall if we want."

"Okay, sure," Queenie replied, tearing open her fruit snacks. "I'll just have to ask my mom."

Erica wiped salt from the corners of her mouth. "Your mom's not the Chinese one, is she?"

"Yeah, she is."

"I always thought you lived with the white one."

"Well, I go to my dad's house practically every weekend."

"Ohhh, okay. Cool."

Queenie nodded.

"So, do you, like, talk Chinese at your house and everything?"

"No," Queenie said, shaking her head. "Never. I don't even know any Chinese. We only ever speak English."

"But weren't you born in China?"

"No, I was born here. And my mom is actually from Malaysia. There's Chinese people there too."

"Oh," Erica said. "Neat." Her lips, irritated by the salt, blushed dark pink.

Queenie inspected a cherry-shaped fruit snack that was missing its stem. Mom would only buy the generic brand, and half of them were always deformed. *What does it matter?* Mom had said when Queenie complained. *Food is food.* Just to get Mom to buy fruit snacks in the first place had been hard enough. *Why do you want to eat this gummy stuff when you could have a banana or a baozi?* Queenie hadn't bothered trying to explain how they traded at recess, and no one would trade for a banana or a Chinese bun. No one would trade for a generic fruit snack either; it had to be Soda-Licious or Gushers. Ryan had once traded a gusher for one of Wendy's paper-thin pieces of seaweed. He and the other boys had laughed as he tore off a little square of the seaweed, opened his mouth wide, and gently placed the square on the tip of his wet pink tongue before curling it back into his mouth. *Eeeeuuch*, he garbled, grimacing. The boys laughed and laughed. Wendy laughed. Queenie laughed too. She left her little saran-wrapped package of baozi in the bottom of her backpack, squished beneath her binder.

"Saturday?" Mom said, not looking away from her own reflection in the bathroom mirror. She was staring at her upper lip, tweezers poised, just as Queenie supposed she'd done with the eyelid hair the day before. "Saturday's no good. Jan asked me to babysit Max for a couple of hours. And I have to do it—no choice. She watered our lawn for two weeks in the summer, remember?"

"So?" Queenie said, looking at Mom's reflection.

Mom pushed her tongue under her upper lip, tilted her head to catch the light. Little black hairs stuck up along the edge of her lip like centipede legs.

"Why does that matter?" Queenie asked, turning away. She couldn't watch Mom doing that, plucking away and looking like a gorilla with her tongue sliding under her upper lip—her *hairy* upper lip. "You can still babysit."

"And carry that crazy baby up and down the mall? Ha, I don't think so."

"You can just drop me off at the mall."

Mom snickered, plucked a hair from her chin.

"I'm almost thirteen now. Everyone else is allowed to go to the mall without their parents."

Aren't you supposed to be at your dad's on Saturday, anyway?"

"He can't on Saturday. He said I was old enough, I should just go to the mall alone."

"I see." Mom put the tweezers back in the medicine cabinet, swung the door shut. "Fine. We'll go to the mall on Saturday. But you're not going alone."

Santa's Village was set up in the mall's main foyer. Kids and their parents lined up behind the red velvet ropes. It wasn't quite noon, and Santa's throne was empty.

Once, when she was little, Queenie had gone with her dad to get a picture with Santa. Santa's Village had looked the same as it did now. She remembered lining up between the velvet ropes, her eyes glued to the curtain behind the throne, where she knew Santa would soon pop out. She'd felt Dad's hand suddenly grip her shoulder, and when she looked up at him, she noticed a man standing beside them, on the other side of the rope. The man was old, with a long grey beard. He wore a tie that looked like the keys of a piano.

"That's a wonderful thing you did there, sir," the man said, tapping Dad on the shoulder. His eyes were light blue, and Queenie could see the whites all the way around. He nodded, looking at Queenie.

"I'm sorry?" Dad said, smiling at the man.

"If it weren't for people like you, I don't know what would've happened to these ones." He patted Queenie on the head with a large white hand.

Dad pulled Queenie closer as the man reached inside his pocket. He retrieved a five-dollar bill.

"Here," he said, holding it out to Queenie. "To show my appreciation. I did my service overseas, mind you, but I never did my part for those poor children over there." He smiled, showing teeth lined with grey gums.

Dad laughed, gently pushed the man's money away. "Oh no, sir. That's not—she's mine. She's my daughter."

Queenie hadn't understood what was happening. She wanted the money; nobody had ever given her five dollars before. She wanted to reach out and take the bill from the man's hand, but she could tell that Dad would get mad if she did.

"Yes, of course she's your daughter. People said we didn't win the war, but was that any excuse to let the children suffer?" The man shook his head gravely, still holding out the money.

"No, I'm sorry, you don't understand—" said Dad.

"Please, I insist. A token of my admiration." The man took Queenie's hand, pressed the five-dollar bill into her palm, and walked briskly away.

Queenie had forgotten about that man until now. Remembering him made her jaw clench up.

"Where is this show supposed to be?" asked Mom, as they paced through the mall. She carried Max on her hip, because she hadn't wanted to ask Jan to borrow her stroller. *I shouldn't be taking the baby to the mall, anyway*, Mom had said. She held Max like a sack of vegetables, one arm around his back, her hip sinking under his weight.

"I don't know where. Erica didn't say."

"Well, what are we doing, then? Where do you want to go?"

"I guess we'll just walk around. We'll probably see it."

Mom sighed. She shifted the baby's weight higher on her hip, quickened her pace. They came to the end of the hallway, turned left. For a brief moment, Queenie considered the possibility that there wasn't any fashion show.

"You carry him for a while," Mom said, putting Max in Queenie's arms. Mom rubbed her lower back. "*Ai ya*, I told you I can't carry this baby around like this."

She continued walking, Queenie trailing close behind. Here at the mall, without the baby, Mom looked different from at home. Hunched. Small. Her shoulders curved, her arms dangled. She looked like a small old lady as she walked through the mall's grand, white-tiled hallways, past all the mannequins wearing leather skirts and silk blouses and tight jeans and T-shirts with *Guess* spelled in sparkly rhinestones. Passing, but not looking. Mom wore white sport socks with her shiny black shoes; you could see them because her pants were too short. Her pantlegs flapped around her ankles.

They passed a girl sitting at a jewellery booth and wearing huge hoop earrings and bright-pink lipstick. Queenie suddenly wished she hadn't worn the T-shirt she had on. She had saved it for this day because it was her favourite: a souvenir T-shirt with a killer whale jumping above the word *Vancouver*, which was printed in glittery letters. But now it felt stupid, kiddish. And it wasn't the right shape—square and too big, not like the tight, stretchy shirts that Erica always wore. Queenie pulled her unzipped fleece jacket closed over her shirt, tucking it under the baby, but then, she didn't like the feel of the fleece jacket either. It was lilac, with a little squirrel stitched into the chest. She shifted the baby to her left side to cover the squirrel.

The stage came into view as they approached the food court. An audience filled the first three rows of chairs, adjusting themselves in their seats and taking off their coats. Queenie sat at the back with Mom and Max as the dance music started. Red and blue lights flashed on the stage.

Erica was the first girl to step out, but Queenie didn't recognize her until she had sauntered halfway across the stage in her white high heels. Her curly hair was poofed up, bouncing about her shoulders as she walked, and her bangs were styled in a swoop across her forehead. She wore a denim jumpsuit. The whole thing was one piece, and it had a big shiny silver zipper right down the middle, zipped up from her crotch to the V-neck at her chest. It was so tight that it looked like her skin was made of denim. The taut fabric hugged her small breasts. She stood in the middle of the stage, one hand on her hip, showing gleaming white teeth between her bright-red lips.

"That's her," Queenie whispered to Mom, pointing Erica out. Mom only nodded as the lights danced over her expressionless face.

Queenie couldn't help but wonder what Erica's skin felt like beneath the denim. She thought of Erica's bare white legs fuzzed with those tiny delicate hairs. She thought of Erica's panties, the skin showing through, the little red hearts disappearing into the shadow where her thighs came together.

Queenie sat through the remainder of the fashion show, not noticing when Mom took the whining baby out of the audience. When the music ended and the lights faded, she spotted Mom way off to the side of the stage area, sitting at an empty table in the food court with Max wriggling in her lap. She looked tired, fed up.

"Your friend was really good," Mom said over Max's crying, her head dodging his flailing fists. "Do you want to go talk to her?" She pointed to an area behind the stage where Erica was standing with a girl, another model. They were both smearing sticks of pink Lip Smacker across their mouths.

Queenie approached them, smiling at Erica, though unsure whether *this* Erica, the model in the skin-tight denim jumpsuit, would even know her.

"Oh," Erica said. "Hi." She looked Queenie up and down, glanced at the girl next to her.

"You were so good," Queenie said, pulling her jacket closed and hugging her ribs. Up close, Erica's eyes glowed sky blue beneath the dark furl of her fake eyelashes. Queenie could only glance at them and then look at the ground. She was afraid her cheeks were red. Erica was wearing green eyeshadow.

"Thanks." Erica tossed her hair. "Actually, I don't get a break like I thought. I have to stay here. Sorry."

Queenie shrugged, still smiling. She felt like a dwarf standing in front of Erica, whose white high heels lengthened her like bubble gum stretched into a thin strand. Queenie looked down at her own thighs draped in baggy corduroy, at her old running shoes, once white but now yellowish grey, scuffed along the toes and riddled with dirty cracks. "I guess I'll see you at school, then."

"Yep. Bye."

Queenie stood there, staring. Max's babbling cut through the ambient noise behind her.

Erica bit her nail, stared back. Then she turned to the girl beside her, asked her if she wanted to go back to the dressing rooms.

When Queenie turned around, Mom was coming toward her with the baby. Max had grabbed the breast pocket of Mom's shirt and was pulling, pulling, making bare skin blink between her buttons. Mom ignored him, kept on walking straight ahead, straight toward Queenie.

The hair had grown back. Queenie could see it, black and coarse, sticking out of Mom's eyelid like a cockroach antenna. It was thicker than before, Queenie was sure. She wondered how long it would grow this time. She wondered how long it would take for Mom to notice, wondered if Mom ever looked, *really* looked at herself in the mirror.

Queenie had dreamt about the hair. In her dream she saw Mom with the tweezers in front of the mirror. But when Mom pulled on the hair, it didn't come out; it kept getting longer. It had been hiding beneath the skin, its full length reeled up in a little ball inside her head, and as she pulled on the end, the hair unravelled. She pulled and pulled, drawing out the wiry black hair like thread from a spool. She drew it out until her arm couldn't stretch any farther. The hair dangled listlessly, reaching almost to her knee.

For breakfast, Mom put a cold shrimp bun on a plate and sat down next to Queenie, who was eating her cereal at the kitchen table.

"Are you going to your dad's this weekend?" Mom asked. She took a large bite of bun. Crumbs fell to the table. She chewed with her mouth open, pressing an oily finger to the crumbs and then shedding them off onto her plate.

"I dunno. He hasn't called." Queenie stared into her cereal bowl.

"Well, it's been three weeks," Mom said. She looked at the calendar on the fridge. "More than three weeks. You can call *him*, you know."

Queenie shrugged. "It doesn't matter." She looked at Mom bending over her plate and shoving the bun in her mouth.

Mom finished chewing, narrowed her eyes. "Why are you looking at me like that?"

"Like what?"

"Like *that*. Like I have something on my face."

"Well, you do. You have that hair again." Queenie pointed to her own eyelid. "There."

Mom touched the hair. She sighed. "It just grows back, always grows back."

She left the house after breakfast without bothering to pluck it out.

Queenie was the champion, and now they called her that for two reasons: she got to the cubbyhole first for the fourth Friday in a row, *and* she was undefeated in the staring contests they had been doing every recess. She had beaten Wendy, Sam, Nora, Becky, Travis, Jesse, Ryan, and Graham, and now she was up against Erica. Erica hadn't wanted to do it—*I'm the best at staring contests, we have to learn to stare in modelling, I'll just beat you, I know I will, I don't want you to feel bad*—but finally Ryan and Jesse had convinced her. Ryan promised Erica three Gushers if she won.

Now they all crowded in the cubbyhole, surrounding Erica and Queenie. Erica stood right in front of Queenie, so close that Queenie could see the little cracks in her lips filled with caked lip gloss. Her breath smelled like sour cream and onion. The skin along her jaw was so white and smooth that Queenie would have believed it was just bone, not skin at all. The dim light that shone into the cubbyhole covered only half her face; the other half was shadowed, darkening her eyelashes and making her blue eyes gleam.

"Ready?" Ryan asked.

Queenie nodded.

"Okay, go!"

Queenie opened her eyes wide, stared straight into the blue of Erica's. Tiny gold flecks swam around Erica's irises. Queenie felt goosebumps creep over her body.

Erica's eyes held for a moment, then dropped away.

"Oh my god!" she cried suddenly. "You've got little hairs there!" She pointed at Queenie's chin.

"What?" Queenie said quietly. "No, I don't." She felt her chin with her fingertips.

"Yeah, you do! Little black hairs. It's like a beard." Erica squealed, started laughing, still pointing. The others started to laugh too. They all tried to look at Queenie's chin.

"Don't," said Becky, trying to hide her smile with her hand. "That's mean."

Queenie didn't know if she should say something, or what she should say. She didn't know if she should ignore Becky or look sad or walk away or get angry or say *Yeah, I knew those hairs were there.* But she didn't do any of those things. She just laughed too. Laughed along with the others, along with Erica, tried to copy the sound of her giggling, the look of her open mouth.

Thieves

WE MOVED INTO THE HOUSE WITH THE MILK CHUTE after my parents' divorce. It was an old wood-sided bungalow on Vienna Drive, painted turquoise with flaking white trim. At ten years old, I was indifferent to the house, indifferent to my new stepdad, but enchanted by the milk chute. In my mind, milk chutes could not exist in Canada; they belonged to the magical world of England, along with candy-red double-decker buses and hundred-room palaces and fish and chips wrapped in newspaper, blackening shiny fingers. England: where my parents fell in love.

My mum had never said much about her life with my dad in England before my sister and I were born, but she had told us that milk was delivered to them in glass bottles, right to their very own chute, and floating at the top of each bottle was a layer of cream. Thick as butter, her guilty pleasure on Tuesday mornings. Unless, she said with a sour edge on her voice, someone else got to the cream first. My dad, sneaking out of bed before she was awake to steal the cream for himself.

◆

I'm driving down the highway, alone and on autopilot, on a mission to get home before my eyes close for the night. The radio whispers with a lilting British accent, "when milk was still delivered to homes in glass bottles ..." I crank the volume.

It's a man's voice. I've missed his name and his reason for being on the radio, but his voice is enough. I let him tell me a story.

A curious string of cream thefts began in England in the 1920s, he tells me. The locals of Southampton began to notice that when they fetched the freshly delivered milk bottles from their doorsteps, the caps had been pried, and the coin of floating cream had been stolen. The thefts continued for some time before a group of amateur birdwatchers finally solved the mystery. It turned out that a species of small bird called blue tits had somehow learned to pry the cardboard lids off the bottles using their skilled little beaks. Then, turning their beaks into drinking straws, they consumed the thick skin of cream.

◆

Our milk chute had fallen into disuse years ago. A board had been nailed over the opening on the inside of the house and painted white to blend into the walls. My mum explained that the former owners had likely boarded it up to keep out the draft, but there would have been a wooden panel set into the wall that you could slide open to retrieve milk bottles. At the other end of the chute, the little door that had once opened from the outside had been nailed shut as well, but the rusty handle remained—evidence that at one time long ago, a real live milkman had opened the door every week to place his delivery inside, and at the other end, someone (perhaps even a girl like me) had slid back the panel to find two precious milk bottles waiting, pooling condensation. The girl wouldn't have needed to see the fingerprints still set in the frosted glass to know that someone had just been there. The same man as always—or maybe not the same man, but it made no difference. As quaint and ceremonial as the exchange seemed, it wasn't magic. It was as real as a stranger coming into your house without saying hello and leaving before you had a chance to think about it.

Even so, I envisioned the milk chute as a secret portal. Every afternoon, when I came home from school, I passed by the little door, eyeing the rusted handle on my way to the back gate. I'd stop, creep closer, close enough to see the grain of the ancient wood, ghostly beneath layers of paint. And as I curled my fingers around the handle, I imagined the door opening into a dark world. Through the chute, a narrow path blanketed in fallen pine needles. Tangled bushes and gnarled trees growing wildly on all sides, slivers of light piercing through the dense canopy above. A labyrinth, beckoning me to explore its depths.

Touching the handle always left the dirty smell of iron on my fingers.

◆

Initially, the ornithologists who studied the blue tit phenomenon explained the cream-stealing behaviour through the theory of "observational learning." One of the birds had, by some fluke, discovered it could pry the lids from milk bottles in the same manner it pried bark from trees to eat the insects beneath. As other birds observed the reward being reaped, they began imitating the behaviour, progressively passing the knowledge from bird to bird until all the blue tits in the region knew the trick.

"That makes sense," I say out loud, as I sit waiting at a red light. But the man insists it isn't that simple.

Blue tits are home-loving birds, he explains. They rarely travel more than a kilometre away from their nests. The ornithologists were therefore puzzled when they discovered that cream thefts had begun occurring in other parts of Britain, in faraway cities, and even as far as Holland.

◆

The man who became our stepdad was nothing like our real dad. Leo's boxes were waiting on our front step the same morning my mum took possession. He was in his twenties—eleven years younger than her. He was tall and wiry, smoked cigarettes, wore leopard-print underwear, and laughed at everything my sister and I said, even when it wasn't funny. He made clam linguini from scratch and taught us how to build a bonfire and watched cartoons with us on Saturday mornings. He told my mum he loved her right in front of us.

My dad refused to refer to Leo by his name. "Him," he called him, as if it didn't matter who Leo was. In my dad's eyes, Leo was every other man—an unknown man, a different man, a man who had stolen his place.

The house we grew up in, where my dad still lived, became empty, cold, as though an invisible frost were creeping over the walls, ever so slowly sealing it up like an igloo. Scars in the carpet marked the phantom shapes of my mum's coffee table, bookcase, nightstand. I wore socks all the time, never letting my bare feet touch the floor. My way of saying, *I no longer belong here.*

For many years, Leo's name was taboo within my dad's house, even when our aunts came to visit for the weekend with a barrage of questions: *Is he nice to you? Is he nice to Mum? Does he hit Mum? Do you call him Daddy? Does he hug you? Does he touch you?* But when we left our dad's house on Sunday night and passed through the door of the house on Vienna Drive—*our* house—he was Leo once again, and there he was, smiling, pouring cream into a steaming pot of clam linguini, and we smiled back.

The year I was eleven, we had a second summer in September. It was the first day of grade six and warm enough to wear shorts. Dry leaves clung to branches, baking in the heat, and the rotten-sweet smell of wilting flowers hung in the air. My sister was in middle school and had gone to a friend's house, so I walked home alone under yellow leaf canopies, back to our house on Vienna Drive.

I took the path on the side of the house like always, by habit reaching out to pull on the milk chute's handle as I passed. But when I felt for the cool metal, it wasn't there. The old milk chute door was gone. In its place was an open space, filled with nothing but air. I peered through the opening. I could see a banister and a staircase, each step edged with gold, peeking out at me. At the base of the staircase was a figure fully cloaked in black, extending a single green arm. Inside was stillness. For a brief moment, I was staring into a parallel universe, about to reach through the space between this world and another. I would need only to hold my breath, step through the portal, and climb the staircase to see how life could be completely different.

And then I realized: I was looking at *our* banister, *our* staircase. Leo's black ski jacket hung on the end of the banister, one sleeve pulled inside and dangling out the unzipped front, baring the coat's green fleece lining. I had not discovered a portal; it was only an empty space. A hole in the wall of our house.

The back door was propped open with my mum's potted geranium. I thought first of the cats, pictured them scurrying down the alley, afraid of their freedom. I wondered what Leo could be doing that warranted knocking out the milk chute and leaving the door wide open. Not until I ventured inside did I consider the possibility that someone else, a stranger, might be responsible.

The house was silent. Closets open, linens torn out and hanging like limp flags. A jar of change was knocked over on the kitchen floor, pennies strewn in a wide arc. Our TV lay smashed on its face at the bottom of the basement stairs. Dusty bootprints stamped into the hardwood. I tiptoed from room to room through the evidence, hearing echoes of what had happened.

"Get out of there," my mum said over the phone when I called her. "Now. Go to the neighbours'. I'm calling the police."

I hung up and ran, through the backyard and across the alley and into the neighbours' yard, all the time telling myself not to look behind me. What would have happened if I'd seen the thieves there in our house, stomping on our floors, rooting through our things? It was possible, even probable, that there'd been only a small window of time between the robbery and my arrival. A space of mere moments between me and the faceless thieves.

◆

I sit in the car on the driveway of my house, watching snowflakes melt on the windshield. It's cold with the heat off, but I'm unable to tear myself from the story on the radio. The man explains that when World War II began and the Germans invaded Holland, all milk delivery abruptly ceased. This made milk and especially the luscious cream floating at the top of the bottle a luxury for humans and a legend for the blue tit. They only live for a year or two on average, and the harsh winters of the '40s ensured that none could survive past this expectation, so all the blue tits who had learned to open milk bottles would have died during the war, giving way to a new generation of birds who had never known the taste of stolen cream.

But when the war ended and milk delivery was briefly revived, the new generation of blue tits once again began stealing cream. To make matters more puzzling, the rate of cream stealing was exponentially higher than it had been before. It seemed that almost instantly, all of the blue tits knew how to perform the trick, and an epidemic of cream thefts erupted.

◆

My sister was promptly sent to the neighbours' house to check on me, and we stayed there until evening, when my mum came to the door wrapped in a pink blanket, glowing against the dark night, her face drawn and flushed. She looked like a victim of fire rather than of robbery. She told our neighbour she was grateful he'd been able to watch us and explained that the robbers had broken in through the old milk chute—could he believe it?

"Crazy," he agreed. "I mean, a milk chute … they're not very wide. I'm sure the guy had a helluva time squeezing himself through."

I imagined a skinny man in ripped black jeans and a black leather jacket, a lit cigarette drooping from his thin lips. He used a laser to carefully cut the hole in the chute, burning through each nail along the edges until the door fell right out, emitting little wisps of smoke as if to signal its defeat. Then, he slid into the opening with his arms stretched above his head, his shoulders butting up against the sides. Twisting his whole body, leather squeaking against the chute's glossy white paint, he squeezed in, millimetre by millimetre. His bones scraped the wooden edge, but he kept writhing, drawing his shoulders in tight, sucking in his breath, thinking, *So close, just a little farther*, and then—*pop*—he was in. His ribs grated the lip of the chute as he pulled his torso through, feet dangling for a moment before he dipped to the floor and slithered in with the skilled silence of a professional prowler.

I had never imagined a robbery so elegant.

Later that night, we all sat in the living room, listing what was missing, sipping hot chocolate.

"Who would do such a thing?" my mum kept asking. "Why would they choose us? And destroy the TV, for god's sake …"

She didn't say it, but we knew what she was thinking. She was wondering if the robbers knew us. If they were out to get us. Maybe they weren't strangers at all.

"I bet they were kids," Leo said. "Just some idiot kids out for a thrill."

It was then that I realized that the robber I'd been imagining, the man I kept picturing over and over again, squeezing his way through our milk chute, looked exactly like Leo.

By the middle of the century, cream thefts were occurring all over Holland. Scientists were having a difficult time explaining the accelerated rate of spread given the large time gap between the first generation of thieves and the current generation. Some even posited that it was impossible to explain by direct transmission and, thus, was evidence of a kind of telepathy, as if the birds were linked by some unmeasurable cosmic force. The man talking on the radio seems to agree. His theory is that when animals acquire a new skill, they involuntarily transfer the knowledge to other animals of the same species as a collective memory, and humans are no different. Consciousness, he suggests, extends beyond the insides of our heads. We are linked to each other in ways we cannot see—shaped by ghosts that were never part of our lived experience but are, none-theless, just as real.

We had another break-in at our house one week later. This time, the thieves bashed in the front door. They didn't take anything. They left a cigarette stub smushed into the floor and a small black hole beneath, burned into the wood like a calling card. In the kitchen, a muffin—removed from its plastic package in the breadbox—sat on the countertop with one clean bite missing from its crusty brown top. Instead of sharing my mum's horror—*Was it them again? The same people? What did they want?*—I felt nothing. It didn't matter who the thieves were. Thieves were thieves. Could you even call them thieves, I wondered, when our house was still the same, every-thing in its place? They were here, and now they were gone. And soon after, we got a new door to cover the open space they had made.

"Sturdier than the old one," my mum said, "and it'll keep the draft out." A new door to cover the evidence that our house was not secure, but permeable. Walls like sieves; find a hole and enter.

Love/Cream/Heat

WHEN LOUISA PULLED UP TO THE HOUSE, her mother was standing on the driveway. She was holding a green cooler and an electric carving knife in one hand and an antelope head by the horn in the other.

"Mom," Louisa said, as she opened her door, "you look crazy."

"Hi, sweetheart," her mother said, setting down the cooler and balancing the knife and the head on its lid. "Give us a squish."

Her face wasn't red or puffy from crying, but as they came together for a hug, Louisa could not help but notice that her mother's fingers, under the nails, were blue.

"How you doin', Mom?" Louisa said into her mother's woolly shoulder, which emanated some vanilla-choked perfume Louisa had never smelled on her before.

"I was just cleaning some things out of the garage," her mother said. "No sense waiting for you and Cole when there's just so *much*."

"Cole's not here yet?"

"Sunday morning," she said. The day of the funeral.

"Bastard," Louisa muttered.

"I know. You probably heard *she* isn't coming." Cole had moved to Singapore with his wife eight years ago, suddenly ordaining Louisa as the recipient of daily phone calls from their mother about suspicious moles, suspicious neighbours, computers that hated her, and the latest garage sale finds. Their mother's resentment over being robbed of her favourite child expressed itself in her refusal to call Mei-Ling by name.

"I'm happy you're here. It's a little unnerving being by myself in this big house." She passed the cooler and the knife to Louisa and hooked her arm around the neck of the antelope. "Now help me get this stuff to goodwill, please." She gestured to a half-empty box sitting at the curb.

"Mom. Poor people don't want Dad's dead animal heads."

"Well, I don't know. I can't exactly throw them away. They remind me too much of him." She turned the antelope's face toward herself and studied it at arm's length. "It's the eyes, I think. So pensive."

Louisa knew that grief came in waves, but it bothered her that her mother seemed so resigned already to her father's death, as though he'd been long gone for years. They busied themselves with sorting through his things well into the evening, and by the end of the day, her mother had yet to shed a single tear. Once Louisa had retreated to her old room for the night, she took out her phone and googled "stages of grief." Most of what she found confirmed things she already knew. Denial, anger, bargaining, depression, acceptance. But was there such a thing as progressing too quickly? Louisa doubted it was truly acceptance if you skipped some of the stages to get there.

Her mind began to wander back to Michener. She'd spent the entire drive to Saskatoon like this, drifting in and out of memories of their time together. What she'd loved most about Michener was his rice cooker. It was the most intimate part of their relationship. Two cups of rice, three and a quarter cups of water, seventeen minutes. It was the only thing they could cook, so sometimes, after sex, they'd sat on the carpet in his dorm room and eaten it by the bowlful, topped with chunks of butter and soy sauce drizzled from little plastic packets. The steam from the cooker hung in clouds around them. What did they talk about? She couldn't remember now. But it hadn't mattered. Common interests were of little concern back then. It was all about fucking, even though fucking was five minutes of missionary on a twin bed, she practising her breathiest moan with each clumsy thrust. Michener always pulled out at the last moment, despite Louisa's being on the pill.

"Sorry," he'd say, finishing himself off while she wiped up with a sock.

Now, after almost twenty years, Louisa found herself longing for Michener. She'd barely given him a thought after they'd parted ways. She knew he'd married the woman he began dating right after her. Rebound Rayleen, Louisa and her friends had called her. Rayleen was pale and wafer thin and considerably taller than Michener, so they made a comically mismatched pair. They'd been only twenty-one. There was a good chance they were divorced by now. He'd stopped posting on Facebook years ago, which suggested he didn't have much to be proud of.

Louisa closed her browser and clicked on the Facebook Messenger app.

Hi Michener, it's been a while! I hope you're well. I'm in town and wondered if you might be interested in catching up? I know a good place for rice. ;)

She stared at the words for a while, reading and rereading and imagining what Michener would think when he saw it. Was it too provocative? Or not enough? She thought of that sly little smile of his, the one that always came on his face when they were taking off their clothes. In the end, she deleted the winky face and hit send.

◆

Cole wrestled with his tie and jacket in the car on the way to the funeral home. His plane had been delayed, so he'd swept in only just in time for the service.

"Must be nice." Louisa drove, eyes on the road.

"Yeah, this is nice," he replied, smoothing his hair in the mirror. "Do you know what a nervous wreck I've been? I've had zero time to process anything."

"Me neither. Our mother is in full purge mode. It's weird. It's like she feels liberated or something."

"It was a long time coming, I guess." Cole sniffed. It took Louisa a few moments to realize that tears were dripping silently from his cheeks and landing on his shirt.

"Cole," she said. "It's okay. You'll wreck your shirt."

"It's not fucking okay," he said.

At the reception after the funeral, Cole wolfed down three egg salad sandwiches, a pile of browning fruit, two oatmeal raisin cookies, and a slice of lemon meringue pie. Louisa couldn't eat. She dabbed at her swollen eyes with fraying tissues.

"So many sandwiches," their mother remarked, as the guests filtered out. "We'll be eating sandwiches until next week!" She clapped her hands.

Cole sat in a chair in the corner of the hall, his legs stuck out in a *V* in front of him.

"You okay?" Louisa asked, tapping the sole of his shoe with hers.

Cole said nothing at first, staring off into the distance. Then: "Is she ... *blue?*" he asked. He was looking at their mother as she hugged the last of the guests.

"You noticed too? Her hands?"

"Yeah. Her hands, but all over too. Look at her face, for Christ's sake."

It was true. Louisa hadn't noticed until now. It was probably the black dress she was wearing, or maybe the fluorescent lighting, that was bringing out the blue tinge of their mother's skin.

"You ask her," Cole said. "I'm just ... exhausted."

Louisa rolled her eyes. "Because you're the only one."

"You don't understand," Cole said, rubbing his face in his palms. He looked up at Louisa with bloodshot eyes. "Mei-Ling is pregnant," he said.

"Oh," she said, pulling up a chair next to him. "Wow. That's ... great!"

"No. No, Louisa, it's not great." Cole rubbed his face again.

"Okay. Sorry."

"We agreed not to have kids. Neither of us ever wanted them."

"Yeah, I know. So was it an accident?"

"I don't know. She says it was. But then I found six unopened packs of birth control pills in her bedside table."

"Jeez," she said. "But wait—how do you know? I mean, it doesn't necessarily mean she deliberately stopped taking them. They could just be ... extra."

"I know. But I just have a feeling. Plus, she refuses to get an abortion."

"What? Why?"

"I don't know! She said something like now that the thing is in there, she just can't bear to get rid of it."

"What a bitch."

Cole glared at her. "Not helping."

"Well, what're you gonna do?"

"I dunno." He sighed. "Maybe ... maybe move back here for a bit."

"Cole. Come on. You're not thinking about abandoning your pregnant wife, are you?"

"Fuck. Just because she's pregnant, now she can be completely manipulative and I just have to go along with it?"

"She's your wife, Cole. You made a vow."

"Since when do you take that stuff seriously?"

"I don't. I just mean that this isn't some girl you knocked up. You're not eighteen anymore."

"I didn't sign up for this!" he said, standing and raising his hands in the air. "Plus my dad just fucking *died*. And I was way the hell in another country."

Their mother turned to him then, raising a hand to her mouth. The lingering guests made a quick exit, eyes downcast. Cole stormed out after them.

◆

It was three days before she received a reply from Michener.

Hey Lou, long time no see! I've been thinking about you, actually. Would love to hang out.

Louisa felt a rush of heat in her groin as she read the message. That he clearly didn't know she was in town for her father's funeral and, therefore, she wouldn't have to talk about it was a relief that felt fervid enough to be erotic in itself. She imagined kissing Michener wetly, pressing him up against a wall.

Tomorrow night? she wrote back.

They arranged to meet at the Silver Dragon downtown. As soon as Louisa was shown to a vinyl booth in a dingy corner of the restaurant, she felt overdressed in her leopard-print dress with a scooped neckline. Michener had not yet arrived. She ordered a bottle of Tsingtao and waited, picking at the label. She tightened the straps of her dress to cover a bit of her cleavage.

He showed up seven minutes late, wearing jeans and a Rough-riders jersey. He smiled and waved as he came toward her.

Fat, was the first thought that came to her. She immediately felt ashamed. Her mind raced with regret over her outfit; why hadn't she just dressed in jeans like she usually did?

"Green machine!" she said, letting him give her a tentative sweaty hug with one arm.

"Yeah," Michener chuckled. "How are you? You look great." He kept looking down at the table.

"Aw, thanks. You too."

He sat down and plucked at the sleeves of his jersey to untuck the fabric from his armpits.

This had been a bad idea. A terrible idea. Any desire Louisa had felt for Michener had completely dissolved the moment she saw him. He looked like a dad—like the dad of someone they would have been friends with back when they were going out. Evidently, he was uncomfortable too; he'd picked up the laminated menu and was examining it, flipping through the pages.

"I haven't been here in a while," he said. "Is it still the same?"

"I'm not super hungry." Louisa slapped her menu face down on the table. "We don't have to eat."

"Oh," he said, setting his menu down on top of hers. "But maybe we should at least get something small? They have fries here, I think."

Fries. Fries at a Chinese restaurant. Her Chinese relatives on her father's side would have balked. Louisa felt pathetic, sitting there with him.

"Um, sure," she said.

Michener ordered and added a Coke for himself.

"I'm glad you messaged me," he said, when the server had left. Louisa smiled. Her gut sank. Was he still expecting to have sex? What would she do?

"How's your wife?" she asked. "Rayleen, right?"

"Yeah, good memory. She's good." Not divorced, clearly. Louisa saw now that he wore a gold wedding band. "She's in Toronto on business," he said. "She's away a lot." His finger traced the water ring left on the table from his Coke glass. "And yours? Sorry, I can't remember his name."

"Nate," Louisa said. "I'm not sure, actually. Divorced. Three years ago now." She held up her ringless hand.

"Oh, man, I'm sorry." She could see in the glint of Michener's eyes that it was a small triumph for him.

"Don't be," she said. "I'm not! It's pretty great being free."

Michener pressed his lips together, then rolled them back out with a tiny pop. "I hope I didn't ... uh ... contribute to that. In any way."

"Huh?" Louisa said. "What do you mean?"

She understood now. He did want to have sex. In his mind, she had been pining for him all these years. He was the one that got away.

"Another one, please," she called out to the server, lifting her empty bottle. She had a desperate urge to get roaring drunk. "You wanna do a shot?" she asked Michener.

He laughed. "Nah, I'm good." Back when they were dating, Michener's drink of choice at parties was a mickey of Captain Morgan rum, which he would polish off handily by the end of the night.

"Okay," he said. "Here goes. I've kind of ... wanted to say something to you, for a long time."

Shit, thought Louisa. This was going to be painful. He was going to ask her for sex, just ask her outright, like a sad little puppy dog. She had not come prepared for this. What would she say? Refusing him, seeing the disappointed look on his chubby face, would be too awful to bear.

She would agree. Yes. She would just do it anyway. How bad could it really be? He would be grateful, after all, and that was a bit of a turn-on.

"All right," she said. "But can I just ask you something first?"

"Sure." Michener picked up his Coke and took a sip.

"Does your wife know you're here with me?"

"Yeah. Why?"

"Oh, okay. I just wanted to know if, you know. She was okay with it."

"She's not the jealous type," he said.

"That's good."

The server arrived with the fries and another beer. Louisa ordered a shot of tequila and shoved a fry in her mouth. It burned her tongue.

"Hot," she said, spitting it out. She rolled it up into her napkin. Michener watched her, smoothing his eyebrow. She remembered now that it was a nervous habit of his.

"Anyway," he said. "Uh ... okay. This is awkward."

Louisa took a long swig of beer. She held the bubbling liquid in her mouth, letting it cool her tongue before gulping it down. She imagined how things would start. Michener would kiss her, very softly at first. His lips looked dry and flaky. His hands would press into the small of her back, and he'd grip the underside of her bare thigh, pulling it up on his hip.

"So, I wanted to apologize," he said.

Louisa went blank. She held his gaze, stunned. She could feel her face flushing.

"For things I may have done," Michener added. "Back when we were dating, you know? It was a long time ago, but ... I've just felt bad about it. For a while now."

"I ... I guess I'm not sure what you mean. Apologize for what, exactly?"

His eyes shot up to the ceiling as he scrubbed his hair. "Oh, man, okay. This is hard. I guess I've realized in the last few years that I was a dick back then. So I wanted to apologize for … for forcing you. For forcing you to have sex with me. I know it happened a lot."

"Oh," Louisa said. Her head spun. Was it the beer? As if on cue, her shot arrived. She didn't want it anymore; she remembered now that she'd hated the taste of tequila ever since she puked it up at a party in university. Michener had probably been there.

"You don't have to forgive me, though," he said. "I mean, I know it's pretty unforgivable."

"No, it's okay." Louisa felt angry now all of a sudden. How the tables had turned—he now the assured and righteous one, and she the damaged, pitiable one. She took three fries and munched them. He sipped his Coke, watching her.

Her mind was reeling through the memories of all the times they'd slept together. She could only seem to recall bits and pieces. She had no recollection of any arguments they'd had over sex. She had no recollection of feeling like she hadn't wanted to have sex. Somewhere deep down, though, she thought she remembered a feeling of repulsion—a lump, dense but pliable, like a chewed-up wad of gristly beef that she carried around in her throat all the time but forced herself to ignore. Her impulse now was to yell at Michener, tell him to fuck off with his apology.

"What inspired all this, anyway?" she said instead. "Did you spend your youth fucking hordes of girls or something?"

He flinched at the word *fucking*. His eyes went to his Coke, which he swirled in the glass.

"Well, no," he said. "After you, I married Rayleen. That was it."

She wanted to throw something at him. She could toss the shot in his face. "I think I need to go," she said.

◆

She cried in the cab on the way home, swigging tequila straight from a bottle she'd picked up at a corner liquor store outside the restaurant. In the months before their separation, Nate had kept calling her *frigid* because she wouldn't have sex with him. At the time she'd thought it was because she'd fallen out of love with him. Now, however, she questioned whether it was something else, some past trauma she'd forgotten about, or perhaps blocked out. Had Michener really forced her? She thought about how she'd felt raw sometimes, how it had hurt to sit down …

And then she was back at the funeral, sitting in the front row between Cole and her mother during the ceremony. An elaborate arrangement of stinking lilies spilled over the casket. Louisa had always hated lilies, their sour, festering smell. Even so, she had been grateful the casket was closed. She hadn't wanted to see her father's face hollowed by chemo, his eyelids like brittle shells, waxed shut. In the eulogy, Louisa's aunt, his sister, had described his final days, how he'd greeted her with a smile each morning. How even at the very end, he did not struggle. How he let go, peacefully, without complaint, without protest.

Heads had bobbed across the room, nodding in affirmation of her father's bravery. At the time, Louisa had been numb, nodding along, but thinking back on it now, she wanted to scream. She couldn't help but picture her father, his body flattened against the hospital bed like an empty sac, a smiling fool, as if he were enjoying himself. As if he wanted the pain, craved the burn of toxic chemicals pulsing through his veins. That wasn't bravery, Louisa knew. It was submission. Pure weakness.

When she got back to the house, Cole and her mother were watching TV in the dark.

"How was your friend?" Cole asked, not looking up.

"Fine," Louisa replied. "Hasn't changed a bit."

In the glow of the TV, her mother's skin seemed ultraviolet.

Louisa grabbed the remote and pressed the power button. The screen went black.

"Hey, what gives?" Cole said.

Louisa flicked on the lights. "We need to do something about your skin, Mom. You need to get yourself checked out."

Their mother scoffed. "Excuse me? What, pray tell, is the matter with my skin?" She looked incredulously at Cole, then at Louisa.

"Do we need to do this now?" Cole said. "You haven't even taken off your coat."

"Your skin is *blue*, Mom. Look at your fingers."

She did, then laughed a little. "Oh, that," she said. "You had me thinking something was really the matter."

"It's not okay," Louisa said. "Blue skin is not normal, Mom."

"Oh, please, Louisa. Don't be so dramatic. It's just the colloidal silver."

"The what?" Cole said.

"It's a treatment I've been taking. A mineral supplement."

"Taking how?" Louisa asked. "Like you've been drinking silver?"

"Well, not *drinking*. Just small doses, two tablespoons a day. And the cream, as well."

"You've been rubbing silver cream all over yourself?" Cole said.

"My goodness, you two! It's perfectly safe. Gwyneth Paltrow uses it. They said that a slight bluing of the skin is normal."

"Gwyneth Paltrow is a kook, Mom. I thought everyone knew that." Louisa tore off her coat and pitched it on the chair.

"I know it's controversial," her mother said. "But I believe it. It makes me feel better."

"This is insane," Louisa said. "You're poisoning yourself, you know that? I have to go to bed. I drank too much."

"Speaking of poison," her mother said, sinking back into the couch and turning the TV back on.

"And another thing," Louisa yelled over the audio. "Why aren't you upset at all about Dad? It's like you don't even care."

Her mother gaped at Cole. He shrugged.

"Oh, come on. Don't pretend like it doesn't bother you too, Cole."

"*Lou*-isa Jean." Her mother slapped her thigh with the palm of her hand. "Listen. I'm sorry I'm not a puddle of self-pity, since that's what you seem to want me to be. What can I say? I've made my peace with it. There's no changing it. No sense dwelling on it." She crossed her arms. "No one ever got anywhere by dwelling. You should go to bed."

The next morning, Louisa woke with a pounding headache. She could hear her mother putting dishes away in the kitchen downstairs. She crept into her mother's ensuite bathroom and got a couple of ibuprofens from the medicine cabinet. There, on the shelf, was a brown glass bottle with a screw-top. The label said Silver Supreme in yellow script against a cartoony illustration of a crescent moon and stars. She unscrewed it and sniffed. It smelled like nothing. She tipped the contents down the drain and set the empty bottle back on the shelf.

When she got to the bottom of the stairs, she saw Cole's suitcase by the door. She stalked into the kitchen and found him sitting at the table with a mug of coffee. Her mother was scrambling eggs at the stove.

"Why are you all packed?" she asked.

"Morning," said Cole. "My plane leaves today. Remember?"

"What the hell? You're going back?"

Cole blew on his coffee. "Um, yeah. I do live there, after all."

"What about all that stuff you said?"

Cole sighed. "I was upset, Louisa. I'd just buried my dad."

"My dad too," she shot back.

"Yeah, *our* dad. People are sometimes irrational when bad things happen, you know."

"Clearly. I feel like I'm the only one around here who's not completely irrational."

"Honey," her mother said, holding up a spatula, "I know this is hard for you. But you're being nasty. Just leave your brother alone. He's got a lot to deal with right now."

"Fine," she said. "Have fun dealing with the baby you don't even want."

That was the last thing Louisa said to her brother before he went back to Singapore, back to his normal life. She sobbed in her room for two hours and then regretted not giving him a proper goodbye. But eventually, once she'd packed up her own things and driven back to Winnipeg, settled back into her apartment and back to work, her memory of that week began to fuzz over like everything else, the sting dissipating with each passing day. Instead, other memories began to surface for her. Older memories. Memories of her dad.

Once, back when she was in junior high, she'd asked her dad what being in love felt like. She'd just started dating her first boyfriend, and what she really wanted was some kind of veiled permission to give up her virginity. She worried, however, that her dad might be embarrassed by the question. But instead, he smiled warmly and thanked her for asking him instead of her mother. He told her that love would feel like losing control. It would feel like she would do anything, absolutely anything for the guy.

"To be honest," he said, "it might feel a bit scary at first. You're a strong girl. You like being in control. But with love, you have to just let go."

It was one of her most heartwarming memories of her father. They'd never been all that close, but in that moment, she felt so loved, so connected to him. Now she felt differently about it. She realized now that in his naive fatherly way, he hadn't even considered the possibility that she might want to have sex at fourteen years old. That she would have sex, and that afterward she would feel new on the outside—like the world had shifted into some alternate dimension where the colours were bold and lurid—and yet old on the inside. Carved out and emptied. Surely her father would have said something different if he'd known.

♦

At the end of July, Louisa received a text message from her brother at 2:23 a.m. She'd fallen asleep with her phone wedged beneath her, and the buzz against her ribs startled her onto her hands and knees like a spooked cat. It was the middle of a freak heat wave, and even though she'd shed all of her clothes, she was sweating, her hair sticky on her forehead.

There was no text in the message, just a photo of a tiny red baby on a weighing scale, screaming. The face was ghastly—bloated, frozen in a tortured grimace. It held its fists up by its ears as if railing against its cruel new surroundings. Was it a boy or a girl? Louisa couldn't tell.

Another photo pinged onto her screen. In this one, Mei-Ling was wearing a hospital gown and cradling the baby to her chest, and Cole was snuggled up against her with his hand on the baby's downy black head. They were smiling, Cole more than Mei-Ling.

Congratulations! she typed back. *So precious.* She quickly deleted the last sentence. There was nothing precious about the baby or the parents. Cole's face, in fact, was as repellent to her as the baby's, with its plastered grin, the edges of his teeth peeking out from his top lip with an eerie shine on them, as if they were made of plastic. *Your hearts must be bursting*, she typed instead. But before she could hit send, her phone shut off. She tapped the screen. Nothing. She fiddled with the power switch. A notification came up: *Temperature. iPhone needs to cool down before you can use it.*

Was it really that hot in her room? She was suddenly aware that her sheets were soaking wet. How had she not noticed?

She went to the thermostat. Thirty-two degrees. The AC had crapped out. She flung open the sliding door to her balcony. It was considerably cooler outside. Her apartment had been cooking, stewing in the muggy air trapped from the heat of the day. She stood naked on the balcony, letting the night air chill her clammy skin. She could see, in the patches of sky amongst the dark clouds, a few stars winking over the city lights speckled below. The acrid smell of a deep fryer rose up from an unseen food truck. Someone yelled in the street, drunk or crazy or maybe both, his echoing words indecipherable. Louisa closed her eyes, overwhelmed by her senses in her half-awake state.

Another forgotten memory now crawled its way out of the cracks of her mind: her and Michener licking out their butter-slicked bowls, their tongues chasing the last grains of rice.

"Shit," Michener said, when he opened the cupboard to put away the bag of rice. Louisa looked inside. A scattering of brown pellets. Shit. Rat shit. The pellets were nearly identical in size and shape to the rice they'd just licked up. Her stomach turned, the congealed mass of rice inside flipping like a dreaming body.

She hadn't forgotten. Not really. She'd simply put it all away, tucked it inside, where it couldn't be seen. That way, she could hold on to everything as if it were buried treasure.

All the way over in Singapore, the next day was already nearing its end. Cole was a father now. His world had been altered, for better or for worse. For some reason, Louisa thought of the antelope head that her mother had eventually thrown away. She pictured it now with its blank, glossy eyes, although it was no longer just a head. It was attached to a tiny human body, fists waving in the air.

There's just so much, her mother had said.

the snare. the arm. the guinea pig. the bottle. the bus. the night.

Why keep watching?
Some people watch, that's all I can say.
There is nowhere else to go,

no ledge to climb up to.

—ANNE CARSON, "THE GLASS ESSAY"

I.

THE THREE-LEGGED CAT SHAT IN OUR YARD eighteen times before Simon began calling it a "public menace." It was black, a crusty-looking stray.

"Damn thing even dug up some of my tulip bulbs," he told Mort, our octogenarian next-door neighbour.

"Have you tried coyote piss?" Mort asked, squinting one rheumy eye. "Works great for deer, I heard."

"I've tried it all," Simon said. "All the homemade potions, stone mulch, ultrasound, sprays ..." He shook his head. Mort shook his too.

"You could try a trap," Mort ventured. "I know a few tricks."

Simon dismissed the idea at first, but I could see in his eyes that he was letting it percolate. That evening, as we sat on the couch, me watching *Friends* reruns and him on his phone, I caught in my peripheral vision the word *snare* strewn repeatedly in the cascade of Google results on his screen.

Mom would not have approved, we both knew. But she'd been gone for five months now, and Simon and I had settled into the relationship that made us most comfortable: ward and warden. It would be a stretch to call him a parent; he left me to my own devices, and I left him to his. I was seventeen, after all, and he had been dating Mom for only a year before being unexpectedly, reluctantly (on both our parts) saddled with me.

But the talk with Mort had psyched Simon up, so the next day he went to the other neighbours, knocking door to door. Turned out the cat had been terrorizing sandboxes and leaving rodent carcasses under porches for unsuspecting gardeners. Everyone agreed: something had to be done.

2.

Two nights later, I saw the cat. It was dusk, and the cat's silhouette was like a shadow puppet against the navy-blue glow of the coming night. I'd been watering the ficus in my window, and there it was, ducking the fence, loping its way across our yard on its three legs like a boat on rough seas. I knew that I was expected to intercept it before it could do its business in the mulch around our maple. But I did nothing. I watched it dig with its front paws, scattering mulch in the space left by its missing back leg. Then it squatted on the remaining back leg, pointing its wide black face straight at me. Its eyes were yellow orbs reflecting the porch light.

I once read that domestic cats are only one branch of the genetic tree removed from their African wildcat ancestors. It might have been that fact that made me freeze, or maybe the knowledge of what might soon happen to it, or maybe the memory of the cat that Mom and I had when we first moved to this city, before Simon. We'd gotten him from the SPCA, and we'd picked him from the dozens of other cats because of how lonely and hopelessly rotund he seemed. He was white with black markings like a furrowed brow across his forehead, and Mom insisted we name him Angus because it sounded sad and sophisticated. But he turned out to be an asshole. Mom said it was just the luck of the draw with cats.

Three days after bringing him home, we were back at the SPCA, braving the shaming gazes of the staff as we passed Angus over.

"So, what happened?" the woman at the counter asked. Mom pulled up her sleeve and laid her bare arm there.

"Oh," the woman said, averting her eyes. Scratches ribboned down Mom's forearm, dried blood raised like glue.

Weeks later, when the deepest gashes had finally healed, the skin was rippled like water.

"See this?" Mom said, running her fingers over the scars. "This is a code. Only you and I know what it means."

"Okay," I said, pretending to understand.

"It means we don't take no shit from no one," she explained.

3.

The following week, construction began on the snare. Clad in green slacks and red suspenders, Mort sat whittling sticks at our picnic table with knobbly, tremoring hands while Simon bent over him. Small white flakes of wood gathered in a pile around their feet.

"It's the trigger," Simon explained, when he saw me watching them.

Mort demonstrated the interlocking notches he'd carved into the end of each stick. "You got that wire?" he called out, blowing the wood dust off his handiwork and spraying a few chunks of spit at the same time.

"Yep." Simon retrieved a misshapen wire from the garage. Mort made quick work of twisting the wire into a series of loops and coiling the end back around itself one, two, three, four, five, six times.

"What's that?" asked Simon.

Mort looked at the noose. "It's a noose," he said.

"Oh. What's it do?" Simon pressed.

"It does exactly what you think," Mort said.

By the end of the day, Simon had tied a rope around a branch of the young maple in our yard and pulled it tight to bend the branch down. On the other end of the rope, he'd attached the trigger and staked the bottom end into the ground. The jagged loop of the noose extended from the trigger like a waving hand.

I woke up the next morning to a whooping sound coming from the yard. I shot out of bed and tumbled down the stairs, still half-asleep. I could see Simon through the screen door, hopping from foot to foot like a dancing devil. I opened the door.

"It worked perfectly," Simon said, resting his hands on his hips. It was a muggy, cloudy morning, but the magpies were chirping away as if to congratulate him.

"Did you get it?" From where I stood on the porch in my bare feet, I could see the rope, taut on the tree's upright limb, but not the noose.

"Nope. It's something else," Simon said. "But the point is"—he stuck a finger in the air—"it works. I'm gonna get Mort." He dashed off, sending the magpies scattering.

The sudden quiet put me on edge. A queer feeling settled in my stomach. It reminded me of my great-aunt's funeral when I was six. I went with Mom, even though I'd never even met Great-Aunt Hilda. Mom hadn't known it was open casket because she wasn't on speaking terms with anyone in her family. When we arrived at the funeral home, we found ourselves being herded with Mom's parents and sisters into a little room off to the side, and there in the corner was Great-Aunt Hilda, lying grey-faced beneath a mound of white flowers. She didn't look real; when we got up close, I could see some kind of yellow wax between her eyelashes, and I guessed this was probably how they kept her eyes fused shut. I wondered if there were eyeballs behind the lids, or if they had scooped those out.

Now, alone in the yard with the snare, I descended the stairs slowly. I didn't know if I wanted to look, but I also knew I really wanted to look. There was the rope, getting longer and longer as I descended each stair. My bare feet felt sticky on the concrete.

I'd only half believed Simon until I saw what the snare had caught. Something small, with patches of orange and white and black fur.

A guinea pig. It dangled from the rope, rotating ever so slightly. The noose was cinched around its belly, where a crescent of sliced flesh peeked out, oozing pink jelly. The legs stuck out pin straight. But the worst part was the face, frozen in a lopsided snarl, eyes bulging out of the head like marbles.

It does exactly what you think.

Without really thinking, I reached into the pocket of my robe and got my phone. I had to crouch down to take the photo; it seemed important to capture the whole face. Afterward, I felt dirty, as if I had germs all over me, even though I hadn't touched anything.

By the time I'd finished showering and getting dressed, the guinea pig was gone. The snare had been reset, and Simon was in the house, watching the news and eating a bowl of Corn Pops.

"What did you do with it?" I said.

"What?" Simon said, crunching a huge mouthful. Some milk dribbled from his lips and down his chin. He wiped it with the back of his hand. "Oh," he said absently. "Don't worry. It's like it was never there."

4.

I saw the first ad taped to the glass of the bus vestibule at the end of our street.

LOST

Calico guinea pig. Her name is Sheila. Last seen on Saturday, March 12.

If you see her, you can coax her with carrots (her favourite).

PLEASE CALL 555-2147, her family misses her!

It was printed in black and white, and at the bottom was a grainy photo of Sheila nibbling a carrot. As soon as I saw the photo, I tore the ad from the glass, folded it neatly, and tucked it into my pocket.

The next day, two more ads had been posted in the same spot. The day after that, three, plus two more on the lampposts along our street.

Meanwhile, the cat shit continued to greet Simon under the maple almost every morning.

"It's mocking us," Simon said. "I mean, the thing is crippled and does nothing but make trouble. What the hell's it trying to prove?"

"It won't take no shit from no one," I said. I took out my phone and found the photo of the dead guinea pig. I'd taken to looking at it every once in a while, just to feel the lurch in my stomach.

"What are you doing?" Simon asked. "You're not texting her again, are you?"

"No," I said. I hadn't done that in a while. At first I'd sent a message every day. It started with questions:

Where are you?

We just want to know you're okay.

Are you coming home?

Are you getting my messages?

Then:

We want to help you.

We are here for you.

We will wait.

I am here, waiting.

I won't be mad, I promise.

When you're ready, I'll be here.

I will wait.

And eventually:

I wore your yellow blouse today.

Ketchup Doritos are back.

Starfish can grow their entire bodies back from a single limb.

I saw an empty bottle on the street with your name written on it.

Simon put two raw herrings on a plate and set it gently behind the noose. They sat there, untouched and rotting, for three days before he finally threw them out.

5.

The day before Mom disappeared, we'd had a dinner party at our house for her birthday. Simon had insisted it would make Mom feel better to have some friends over. "Laugh, drink, be merry and all that," he'd said, pinching Mom's butt in the kitchen as she scurried around, garnishing the food and polishing wineglasses.

At dinner, he'd asked Mom what medication she was taking now. "What is it, sex something, Sexela?"

"Celexa?" said Brad, who was a GP.

"All I hear is sex," said Simon. "But we all know that ain't happening."

Brad chuckled a bit, but everyone else looked at their plates.

"I think you've had a bit much to drink!" said Mom, and laughed too loud. Her smile looked painted on.

"She's tried everything," Simon continued. "Prozac, Lexapro, Zoloft—that was a fun one."

"It can be tough to find the right drug," Brad said.

"Anyway!" Tina chimed in, grabbing the wine bottle and pouring herself a generous glass. "Colin finally convinced me to go camping last weekend."

"Really?" said Mom. "How was it?" She looked like a little kid then, her cheeks flushed as her fingers brushed the hair behind both her ears at once, smoothing and smoothing. She was wearing the yellow blouse. She'd told me that she hated it, but the colour was flattering. It had been a present from Simon when they first started dating.

Later, Simon brought out the cake, topped with tea lights because he had forgotten to buy birthday candles. The cake was chocolate ganache, and Simon had decorated it with pink icing hearts and written Mom's name across in script letters. Everyone sang off-key, and Mom blew out the candles.

"It's a beauty, isn't it?" Simon said. He plucked off the tea lights one by one. "Just wait until you taste it."

Everyone was looking at Simon when Mom's hand came up from under the table. No one saw it but me. I saw her hand move in one swift motion to the edge of the glass plate holding the cake and push it. She pushed it to the edge of the table and let it fall to the hardwood floor. The cake landed upside down, the plate stuck to its underside. It made a squelching sound when it landed, like a cartoon sound effect. Pink icing splatted out from beneath. Tina gasped.

"Oh, shit," said Colin.

Mom stood up. "It's ruined," she said, stepping over the cake and out of the room.

Would things have been different, I wondered, if I'd done something then? If I hadn't helped to shuffle the guests out the door, laughing and apologizing while Simon cleaned up the mess in the other room?

Through their bedroom wall, I heard Simon yell, "Why do you insist on making me look like a fool?" I wanted to find the ruined cake, dig my fingers into it, smear ganache all over the white walls for Simon to find in the morning. I looked for the remains of the cake in the garbage, but they weren't there. Simon had flushed it all down the toilet. The glass plate sat empty on the counter, washed and dried and waiting to be put away.

I happened to be looking at the photo when I saw her. I was sitting in the bus vestibule, waiting for the bus, my phone zoomed in on the guinea pig's snarling face. In my peripheral vision, I caught someone on the other side of the glass, kneeling down and reaching into a backpack. When she stood, she was holding a piece of paper in one hand, and four squares of tape were stuck to the fingers of the other. She fixed the poster to the glass and then went about putting up three more before she saw me watching. She gave me a shy smile.

It was snowing a bit, and when she came into the vestibule, she flung back her hood to slough off the flakes. She was around my age, maybe a couple of years older. Her hair was dyed purple, but the blond roots were showing. "You live around here?" she asked me.

"Kind of," I said, clicking off my phone.

Her forehead crinkled. "Okay, well, any chance you've seen a guinea pig?" She pointed at her posters on the other side of the glass. "Some jerk keeps taking my posters down."

My throat felt tight. "You lost your guinea pig?" I said.

"It's my little sister's," she said.

"Oh," I said. "Sorry. She must be upset."

"Yeah."

We didn't say any more. The girl smoked half a cigarette and stubbed it out on the pole as the bus was pulling up. She put the rest in her pocket.

She chose a seat first, and for some reason I sat right in front of her. "How do you lose a guinea pig, anyway?" I found myself saying to her.

"I dunno," she said. "I guess she took it outside and something spooked it. A cat or something. It ran off into the bushes and disappeared. But like, she's five years old, and she absolutely adored that guinea pig. No way we can tell her that thing's never coming back."

"Yeah," I said. "That's hard."

"I hope it's okay, though. My parents keep saying maybe someone found it and kept it or something. I just can't help but imagine the worst. Some kind of horrible, gruesome death."

It does exactly what you think, I thought.

6.

A snowstorm arrived in the middle of April and buried the snare. The snow had blown up against the porch where the maple stood, and the rope, still pulling the tree's limb, disappeared into the white drift.

I saw the cat again that night. From my window I could see it pawing through the snow, sinking to its belly with each step. Simon was asleep, so I crept downstairs and slid my feet into my boots.

There was no sound, no wind, no moon that night. I sat on the porch steps, watching. The cat didn't seem to notice. It sniffed at the snowdrift where the snare was buried. There was no way for it to take a shit there without sinking.

And just like that, the cat conceded. It turned and wandered away, carving a path straight for the gap in the fence.

"I'm waiting," I said as it slipped away.

Kevin Bombardo

WE USED TO JOKE THAT WE'D ALL GOTTEN FAT after only a few months of working at the Belleville Mall Starbucks. "The Frappuccino fifteen," we called it. My drink of choice eventually became an iced quadruple-venti two-pump-valencia non-fat light-ice Americano Misto. I had many reasons to hate myself.

One of them was a guy named Guy. We'd work tandem on bar during the rushes after movies, him steaming and me pulling shots and calling out drinks like tongue twisters, the two of us gliding around each other to pump syrups, drizzle caramel, hip check the fridge door, wipe the steaming wands, blow out the old milk with a sharp hiss of air. It was sexy, in a way, to work so seamlessly together, anticipating the movements of each other's bodies. Nothing was sexy, however, about Guy. Picture him cinched in that green apron, pear-shaped, nasal-voiced, and perpetually sweaty, in contrast to the aloof, tortoiseshell-framed faces of the university student hipsters that dominated our branch. Guy was the oldest of us all, somewhere in his midthirties. But he and I were the only two men at the branch, and we bonded over our love of *The Simpsons*, throwing out quotations and references like inside jokes, at which the other baristas would roll their eyes. "Kippers for breakfast, Aunt Helga?" I'd say, and Guy would return with, "Is it St. Swithin's Day already?" echoing my bad cockney accent.

He mistook it all for flirting. I don't know, maybe it was, but I was twenty-two and therefore oblivious to my ability to control the things I said and did for the sake of others. Somehow, I'd seen Guy as asexual, devoid of human desire, simply because I found him in no way attractive.

When do we stop regretting the people we once were?

Another reason was Kevin Bombardo. I can still picture him perfectly, his sandy bowl cut and dusty coveralls, pushing his custodian's cart across the food court, the wheels thrumming against the tiles. I'd watch him roll on past as I waited in line at the Pita Pit for my spicy Greek. "How's life treating you today, Kevin?" I'd say.

"Like a dirty diaper," he'd groan every time, without fail.

"I hear ya," I'd reply, as if he and I shared the same life.

Truth: Kevin was a daily source of amusement among the baristas. I wasn't the only one who sought him out during my breaks so that I'd have the funniest story to tell about what crazy thing Kevin did today. *He ate a crust from someone's abandoned sandwich! He chased after an escaped toy poodle and caught it in an empty mayo tub! He rolled over the toes of a lady's shoes with his cart and then tried to polish them with his Windex!* Our revelling led to the rumour that Kevin was an "idiot savant," though no one really seemed to know what his gift was. Claire guessed he was a numbers whiz, like Rain Man. Heather said he was a chess grandmaster. Everyone seemed to agree that he was homeless, or at least a drifter of sorts. Why? Maybe it was something about his face, the deep lines carved in his forehead, the shoe-shine of his skin, or the way he moved as though dragging an invisible weight behind him that made him seem time worn and battered, even though he was not old. Or maybe it was simply his imperviousness to judgment that forced us to classify him in a realm of society that was the furthest from our own we could imagine.

Usually, my interactions with Kevin were limited to that three-line exchange; he seemed entirely disinterested in taking it any further. But on one particular day, he actually tried to spark a conversation with me. I was reading a frayed second-hand copy of *Atlas Shrugged* while I ate my pita at a crumb-laden food court table. I heard the rumble of Kevin's cart draw near, then stop. He sat down in the seat across from me.

"Garbage," he said.

I laid the book face down, splayed open. "Oh, hey, Kevin," I said.

"What are you reading that for?" he said. He had a zit on the tip of his nose, with a white bulb sticking out of the centre. I had to look away.

"I just started it," I said, flipping the pages with my thumb. "It's a pretty important book. Pretty long though too."

"I'll save you some time," Kevin said. "Be selfish. Altruism is a lie. Every man for himself."

"Hmm," I said. I'd only read up to page 21 by that point. It seemed like Kevin was trying to tell me something about the book, but then, I had a hard time believing he'd actually read it, and an even harder time shaking the feeling that he was accusing me of something.

"My roommate said this book basically changed his life," was all I could think to say.

"Figures," Kevin said, and went on his way.

I left my tray—strewn with soggy pita wrapper, castaway olives pooling in feta-flecked dressing, and my half-empty iced quadruple-venti two-pump-valencia non-fat light-ice Americano Misto—on the table for Kevin to clean up, like I always did.

When do we stop regretting the people we once were?

"Kevin's in good spirits today," I told Guy when I returned from break. It was slow, a weekday, just the two of us on shift.

"Sporting his signature ketchup stains, no doubt?" Guy said.

"So chic," I said.

Guy was sweatier than usual that day and had been messing up drinks. I should've seen it coming, but I didn't. As we were closing up at the end of the day, he said, "Hey, are you thinking about seeing *The Manchurian Candidate?*"

"Yeah," I said, mopping away around the café tables. "I want to. I heard it's great."

"Cool," he said, hands on hips. "I think we should go, then. I'd like to take you. Friday night?"

My head rushed, a million tiny hot needles pricking all at once. I felt trapped. "Um, okay," I said.

For the rest of our shift, as Guy cashed out the registers and I closed up the bar, I was silent. It was shame piling on top of me, heavier and heavier, as my brain took stock of the implications of what I'd just agreed to. I would have to go on a date with Guy. In public. People would see us together. I might know those people. He would be wearing something tacky, like a tucked-in polo shirt, his round gut propped up at his beltline. He might expect us to hold hands. Or kiss. Or …

He must have sensed my discomfort, because he was silent too. Embarrassed, probably. Had he ever asked out another guy? I wondered. Had he ever asked out anyone before? His chubby cheeks were pink and shiny.

The next day, I chose to confide in Jamie, who worked only once a week because she was in engineering school, but whose Drew Barrymore looks and charisma made her everyone's favourite co-worker.

"Oh my gawd," was Jamie's gleeful response. "I can't believe he thinks he is anywhere close to your league."

"I feel bad," I said, though I didn't. In fact, I felt more confident than I'd felt in a long time. I was proving to Jamie how desirable I was, and Jamie was confirming it. "I don't know how to let him down," I said, continuing my charade of compassion. "But, I mean, if I go on the date, I'll feel like I'm just leading him on."

"Do you want me to say something to him?" Jamie asked. It seemed harmless enough. It would be less awkward for Guy, I reasoned, if he didn't have to face me when I rejected him.

Turned out, of course, it was more awkward, and certainly more humiliating, to be told by Jamie in the backroom while they hauled out bags of mocha powder that I was "really uncomfortable" with Guy's advances. Jamie explained to him that I was just not interested, and that to avoid making it even more uncomfortable for me, he should probably just drop it and move on. Guy emailed me that night at 2 a.m.

Anthony,

*Please be aware that if you need to say something to me, you
can say it DIRECTLY. I've had enough experience in my life to
be able to handle all types of rejection. No hard feelings.*

I read the email over and over, my stomach dropping a little
more each time. I thought about replying, but didn't know how to
muster a defence or an apology. To do either would be to admit
guilt. So instead, I hit forward. I sent the email to Jamie, typing at
the top, *Oh shit, look at the reply I got from Guy! I think he's pissed.*

It was the hot gossip at the store. I got frequent reports from the
other baristas who worked shifts with Guy on how he was doing.
*He seemed pretty depressed; he barely said a word; he was kind of bitchy
to a customer.* Since Guy was a shift lead, it wasn't surprising that
we weren't scheduled together for the next two weeks. Then, all of a
sudden, he transferred to another store.

"Thank god," Jamie said when she heard. "What a creep." I didn't
think Guy was a creep. I thought he was actually a nice guy. I liked
working with him and thought I might even miss his presence, and
yet at the same time, I shared Jamie's relief. With Guy gone, the
whole thing would eventually fizzle away, and I could stop thinking
about it. I could stop feeling the wave of roiling regret that would
hit me at odd times throughout the day, in those arbitrary moments
when the world seemed to throw the past into sharp focus, pulling
me abruptly back into my real body—the body that allowed me to
feel feelings and act accordingly.

Sure enough, it wasn't long before Guy began to fade from my
periphery. Eventually, I left the job at Starbucks, along with all the

friends I'd made there, and began interning at a local lifestyle magazine, where I made new, more artsy friends, including Shannon. She was co-founder of the magazine and had inexplicably chosen me as her protege and confidant, which of course, I flaunted as significant social capital. The two of us went out to see a Noah Baumbach indie film one night. We were standing in line at the concession, sure that were headed for an empty theatre while the philistines around us packed in for the blockbusters. Shannon had just dumped her rotten boyfriend, and I was consoling her as we approached the counter to order. "He's a dickless turd," I said. "End of story." At that moment, the person ahead of us turned around and faced me, Guy, two jumbo bags of popcorn cradled in his arms and two sodas clutched in his hands. We both froze.

"Hey!" I said, a little too loudly. I started to move in for a hug, but luckily the food was in the way.

"Hi," Guy said. He'd gained weight. He did, indeed, have his shirt tucked in. There was an excruciating moment of silence as Shannon slipped ahead and began to order for us, leaving Guy and me alone together. We stared at each other. I could not keep myself from fiddling with my hair, smoothing it against my forehead.

"Well, nice to see you!" I finally said, pointing at Shannon and going to her side, as if I was really needed for ordering popcorn. Guy walked away without a word.

"An old flame?" Shannon said, jabbing me in the ribs.

"Fuck no," I said. We both laughed.

When we got past the ticket booth with our snacks in hand, we found a small crowd of people waiting outside the theatre. "Jeez," I said to Shannon as I scanned the cargo shorts and Hollister

T-shirts milling about. I was just about to joke that the Steven Seagal movie must be all sold out, but stopped short. There was Guy again, standing at the edge of the crowd. "They're just cleaning it," he said when he saw us. His face was flushed—the same rosy cheeks he'd had the day he asked me out. Standing right next to him was Kevin Bombardo.

It took me a minute to recognize Kevin without his custodian's cart; I'd always thought of him and his cart as inseparable, a package deal. But there he was, with his sandy bowl cut, looking exactly the same in every way except for his clothes, a short-sleeved dress shirt and jeans. My first thought was that this was some crazy coincidence: the three of us had just happened to decide to see the same movie, here, on this night. But, no, I quickly realized. They had come together.

"Kevin Bombardo," I blurted out.

He gaped at me for a moment. Did he know me? he was thinking.

"How's life treating you today?" I said, and his face clicked back into position.

"Like a dirty diaper," he said, scrubbing his chin in a way that revealed how habitual this response had become, like a dog performing a trick for the thousandth time. "A Starbucks guy. So you two must've worked together, huh?"

"Yeah," said Guy. "Just for a few months before I moved to Birch Plaza."

"Was it only a few months?" I said. "It seemed more like a year, maybe even longer."

Guy only shrugged.

"How's Birch Plaza?" I asked.

"Oh, I have no idea," Guy said. "I haven't been there for a while. I'm at the Boys & Girls Club now. Community Engagement Coordinator."

"No way," I said. "Good for you."

We both nodded and nodded in the silence, mirrors of each other with our bags of popcorn clutched to our chests. I tried to think of questions to ask about Guy's job, but everything I could think of made me feel like a nine-year-old interviewing his uncle for a school project. *What kinds of things do you do? Do you like it? What's your favourite part?* So I asked nothing. Shannon raised her eyebrows and rooted around in her purse. Kevin stood still and solid as a tree. It didn't even occur to me to introduce them; my mind was too busy obsessing over what Shannon must be thinking about my past associations with such obvious losers and how Guy had managed to get a grown-up job and twisting all of it into clear evidence of my own failure.

"I'm working at *Loom* magazine," I finally announced. "It's pretty cool." Vague on the details, so I could come across as having a real job, like a photographer or a journalist.

"Loom," Kevin said, squinting. "Like weaving?"

It took me a moment to understand what he meant. But it was clear he was not joking. His face was blank, awaiting my answer.

Shannon laughed. "No, not like a loom," she said. "Like looming. When something's about to come."

"Huh," Kevin said.

It was an awful, idiotic name for a magazine, I suddenly realized. It had been Shannon's idea.

"That sounds great," said Guy.

"He's our best intern by far," Shannon said, patting my head like a proud mother. At the time I thought she was trying to alleviate the awkwardness, but even so, it was all I could do not to slap her hand away.

Kevin nodded. "Seems like the perfect kind of job for you," he said, as if he knew me so well.

Mercifully, the doors opened at that moment, and we filed with the crowd into the dark theatre. Shannon and I went down the left aisle, and to my relief, Guy and Kevin took the right. People, strangers, filled in the spaces around us as Shannon and I negotiated where to sit. After we'd settled in with our coats tucked under our seats and our drinks in the cupholders, I saw that Guy and Kevin had somehow ended up sitting directly in front of us, with only one row of empty seats between us.

I couldn't pay attention to the movie. All I could think about was time—how my sense of it seemed so wrong, how years in my mind could be months in someone else's. How seeing Guy could throw me out of myself, even though I was the one who was supposed to have broken his heart. It had only been a few months. *No hard feelings.*

Somehow even more unsettling was seeing Kevin there with him. Kevin out in the world, plucked from his spot in my memory as an object of ridicule and dropped in front of me, a flesh-and-blood human. What had he meant when he said it was the perfect kind of job for *me*? I couldn't help but consider the possibility that if things had gone differently, it could have been me sitting next to Guy. How long had they been together? I wondered. Had Guy changed his mind about Kevin at some point, or had he been pretending all along, joining in on the running jokes about Kevin just to fit in?

Partway through the movie, Kevin put his head on Guy's shoulder, and Guy's head fell naturally against Kevin's, as though their bodies were designed to slot perfectly together. I remember thinking Kevin was lucky then. To have a big, solid shoulder to rest his head on. A resting place, a comfort, devoid of any fear of scrutiny. How people saw it from the outside was meaningless.

When we emerged from the theatre, the night was warm. It jarred me a bit, the dark and the warmth together, the AC chill suddenly absent, and the air thick and dry in my throat. It felt like we'd just come back to Earth from some other planet.

"Man, those guys are such creeps," I said, stealing a glance at Guy and Kevin, walking behind us.

"That much is clear, honey," Shannon said. "The one guy was giving me Buffalo Bill from *Silence of the Lambs* vibes." To hear Shannon dismiss them seemed to set the world right again. Relief rushed through me like a drug.

"Why does everyone suck except for us?" she went on, linking her arm in mine. It was the refrain of our friendship, which could essentially be reduced to Shannon toting me around like Rupert Everett in *My Best Friend's Wedding* while the two of us mocked people to salve our frequently bruised egos.

"Good thing they can't make babies together," I said.

"You're sure he doesn't have one in that gut of his?"

"Nah, god made that one barren for sure," I said. We laughed, throwing our heads back, making a show of how venerable we thought ourselves.

When do we stop regretting the people we once were?

I ended up leaving *Loom* soon after. I got tired of being an intern, and Shannon got tired of taking in new interns as pets, until eventually, without enough free labour, the magazine was a sinking ship. I decided to go back to school. I started taking courses in journalism but eventually switched over to English literature. I collected scarves, wool and pashmina, in a rainbow of earth tones, and wrapped them around my neck each day in a way that I imagined appeared windswept. I started a master's degree and buried myself in research on ekphrastic poetry and illuminated manuscripts. I began to see myself as a serious person.

And then I met Liam. I'd been hesitant about getting into a relationship with him, not because he was a sessional prof and I'd been his student, but because of his kid, whom he shared custody of with his ex-wife. Hattie was just shy of four when I first met her. Liam introduced me as his "very good friend," and Hattie spent an hour or two side-eyeing me over lasagna. When the time came for dessert and I brought out the amaretto ricotta cheesecake that I'd special-ordered from Le Pré Patisserie, rated at five stars on Google reviews and located in the most recently gentrified urban quarter of the city, I was sure I'd win her over. Of course, anyone who knows anything about kids can guess how that went.

"Why's it got dusty grapes on it?" she asked her dad.

"Those are cranberries," I shot back. "Sugar-dusted cranberries," I added, softer now.

"Oh," she said. Then, looking up at her dad, "Can I have a cookie?"

Liam let her have her cookie, onto which she squirted her own design from a tube of blue icing. While she smushed a handful of star-shaped sprinkles into the icing, I carved out two pristine slices of cheesecake for me and Liam.

"Isn't it beautiful?" I said, still half expecting Hattie to change her mind and beg for a slice. But she took no notice, happily licking blue icing from her fingers.

"So beautiful," Liam said, turning the plate around to admire the slice from all sides. "Almost too beautiful to eat." Which turned out to be true, as I saw the white box containing the leftover three-quarters of the cake in the fridge a week later, still neatly taped closed. I hadn't realized it at the time, but Hattie's rejection of the cake had actually been edifying. I'd failed to impress her, but it hadn't mattered to her or to Liam, in the end. We continued spending time together. I fell in love with them both, and they reciprocated. I stopped trying so hard. I moved in and began wearing sweatpants in the evenings. I took up cooking and bought cookbooks with shiny pastel covers and titles like *Yum & Yummer* and *The Art of Simple Food*. And just two years later, Liam and I got married—a choice that my younger self would certainly have scoffed at. Liam's ex ran off to South America with some naturopathic health guru, and we were granted full custody of Hattie. My world shrank to packed lunches, gymnastics practice, bingeing episodes of *RuPaul's Drag Race* on Netflix with a glass of prosecco after Hattie was in bed. I don't mean to make it sound depressing; it was actually the opposite. It felt real, purposeful in a way my life hadn't been before.

But then one day, out of nowhere, there was Kevin Bombardo again. It was a Monday afternoon, and Hattie had convinced me to make a quick stop at a playground on our way home from the market. I was carrying a bag of veggies and a whole salmon on ice that

I'd bought on impulse from a local fresh-caught seafood stand, and I was trying to decide how much longer we had before the ice melted. Kevin rolled across the grass on an old Schwinn bicycle, his bowl cut, sandy as ever, skirting the brim of a tweed flat cap. He wore a trench coat and trousers, and a leather briefcase was strapped with bungee cord to the rack on the back of his bike. He gave me a brief look, which I mistook for recognition.

"Hey, Kevin," I called out. "How's life treating you?"

He didn't respond. He rolled to a stop beside me, scanning the area. I saw then that a pair of cordless earbuds were nestled into his ears like pearls. He hadn't heard me.

I just about waved to get his attention, but stopped myself short. I realized that I didn't actually want to know whether or not he remembered me. I had a gut feeling that either way, I'd be reminded of how wrong I was about everything, how naive I'd been to think I'd finally figured myself out.

He leaned his bike against his hip and removed his earbuds, one by one, tucking them into his coat pocket.

Hattie called out. "Uh, Anthony? Help?" She was stranded in the middle of the monkey bars, dangling from her spindly little arms.

"Coming, honey," I called back, grateful for the excuse to move away from Kevin. I set the groceries down on the bench, and in my peripheral vision, I thought I could see his head turn to look at me, but I didn't dare look back. I helped Hattie jump down, and she jetted for the swings, pulling me by the hand. But Kevin stopped me.

"Hey," he said, "your name's Anthony?"

"Yeah," I said, walking over to him. "Hi."

"I knew an Anthony once." He bobbed his head vigorously, as if riding along a bumpy road. "A real fucker."

I just stared at him. I didn't know what to say. I felt frightened, my heart suddenly thudding in my ears, even as I tried to reason with myself that he'd always been a weird guy and was probably just trying to be funny.

"This guy," Kevin went on, "I met him in law school. But I never took the bar exam. Couldn't stomach it anymore, and fuckers like him were the reason."

My eyes shot to Hattie. She was swinging on her belly, watching us. Her eyes were wide, sensing that something was off.

"What did he do?" I asked.

"He was a liar," Kevin said. "The worst kind of liar is the one who lies to himself." He shook his head.

We stood in silence. My mind raced, thinking of how to respond. It was that same feeling I'd had in each of the brief conversations I'd had with Kevin in the past—a feeling that there might be a code in what he was saying, but some deficiency in my character left me unable to crack it. Was he talking about me? Did he recognize me, or was he conflating his memories? Had he really been to law school? I volleyed, certain at first that Kevin had a deranged, manic glint in his eyes, yet struck by how normal he looked, far more polished now than in his custodian days, which led me to believe that what he was saying must be true and that I was an asshole for doubting him. I thought about how I'd never been able to finish my master's thesis and now I was wearing checkered Vans, while Kevin wore what looked like real Blundstones, just barely scuffed at the right toe.

"I'm sorry," I finally said.

Kevin shrugged. "That's how she goes, right? You let down your guard, someone's gonna use you up."

"Like a dirty diaper," I said.

"Exactly," Kevin said, pointing a finger at my face. Then he redirected the finger to my groceries sitting on the bench. "That a fish?" he said.

"Yeah," I said. "Wild sockeye salmon." Suddenly I felt like the worst kind of hipster—the kind who buys wild salmon to make gourmet meals as a hobby while living off his tenure-track-professor husband, blind to his own self-righteousness.

"Hm," Kevin said. "You know, I went fishing once with my kid. We caught a trout, a nice big one. I taught her how to gut it. When I cut it open, there was a mouse inside."

"What?" I said. "How? How did it get there?"

The question seemed to surprise him. He shrugged. "Everything eats mice," Kevin said, without a hint of derision.

I tried to picture the mouse, curled up into a ball, cradled in the fish's flesh, its dark fur slick and wet. "Did you still eat the fish?" I asked.

"Sure," he said. "Lifted the mouse out by its tail and tossed it back in the water. Didn't change the fish."

Hattie approached us then, stopping a good distance away with her feet planted apart, chewing her nail.

"My daughter," I said to Kevin. "Everything okay, honey?"

She nodded. "Can you push me?" she said.

"Of course he can," Kevin said, his face lighting up.

I knew that Hattie had come to save me, not consciously, but by some instinct that had picked up on how helpless Kevin had rendered me. Nonetheless, she looked at Kevin plainly and then smiled. She was only six years old, but it occurred to me then that she'd already become a far better person than me.

"Sure," I said to Hattie. "See ya," I said to Kevin.

"Later," he said. He watched as I followed Hattie to the swings and began to push her, my back turned. I could feel Kevin's eyes on us, but Hattie seemed to have forgotten about him. She let her head fall back, her eyes closed and her face serene as the wind rushed past.

I don't know exactly how long Kevin watched us. I thought about how our places could be switched—Kevin pushing his daughter on the swing on a leisurely afternoon, and me watching from a distance. After a few minutes, I turned around, and he was gone. I pushed Hattie high, her sandalled feet kicking the sky, high enough for her to catch air at the top, her hair floating in orbit around her head for one brief moment.

ACKNOWLEDGMENTS

MY GRATITUDE TO my dear friends and first readers, Alix Hawley and Adam Lewis Schroeder, who helped me chip away at the bulk of these stories. Thank you for the insight, expertise, and unfailing encouragement you've given me for the better part of a decade. Thanks also to Shelley Wood for lending your keen editor's eye to some of my recent work and John Lent for gems of wisdom about writing that continue to stick with me.

To my friends and colleagues at Okanagan College, especially Sean Johnston and Jake Kennedy, whose work I look to with great admiration: thank you for countless inspiring conversations about books and the craft of writing. I am also grateful to the astute editors of the journals in which many of these stories first appeared, for investing the time to help me become a better writer; to all the brilliant writing teachers I've had over the years—Suzette Mayr, Nicole Markotić, Aritha van Herk, Robert W. Gray, and Mark Anthony Jarman—in whose workshops some of these stories had their humble beginnings; and to my students, for challenging me to keep learning along with them. To the many friends and family members who inspired these stories, thank you for allowing me to shamelessly pilfer anecdotes and model characters on you.

To my agents, Samantha Haywood and Marilyn Biderman, thank you for your tremendously valuable editorial suggestions and for cheerleading this book toward a perfect home.

Many thanks to Brian Lam and the entire team at Arsenal Pulp for believing in these stories and for all the hard work you've put into publishing them. Special thanks to Jazmin Welch for the striking book design, Christina Mrozik for permission to use their stunning artwork, and Catharine Chen for her generous, discerning, and meticulous editorial suggestions. It was a great pleasure to nerd out over language in your company.

I wouldn't have had the time, space, or conviction to devote to writing if not for the support of Okanagan College, CBC Books, and the Banff Centre for Arts and Creativity. Thank you for validating and championing the worth of my work as a writer.

And to my family, especially Andrew and Josephine, the centre of my world: nothing would be possible without you.

CORINNA CHONG received her MA in English (Creative Writing) from the University of New Brunswick. Her first novel, *Belinda's Rings*, was published by NeWest Press in 2013, and her reviews and short fiction have appeared in magazines across Canada, including *Grain*, *Ricepaper*, *Room*, *Riddle Fence*, *The Malahat Review*, and *PRISM international*. She won the 2021 CBC Short Story Prize for "Kids in Kindergarten." She's currently working on a novel called *Bad Land*, set in the Canadian badlands of Drumheller, Alberta. She lives in Kelowna, BC, on the traditional and unceded territory of the Syilx/Okanagan people, where she teaches English and fine arts at Okanagan College.

corinnachong.com